The Echo

Also by Giles A. Lutz:

The Echo

GILES A. LUTZ

DOUBLEDAY & COMPANY, INC.

GARDEN CITY, NEW YORK

1979

Library of Congress Cataloging in Publication Data

Lutz, Giles A
    The echo.

    I. Title.
    PZ4.L976Ec [PS3562.U83]   813'.5'4
    ISBN: 0-385-15403-8
    Library of Congress Catalog Card Number 79-7120

acc'd
3-80

The Echo

Prologue

There are events that occasionally happen that are so mind shattering that man never fully recovers from them. The duration of the experience does not matter, be it a brief flick of time, or a never-ending hell. His mind is forever burdened, and no matter how he struggles, he cannot seem to free himself.

Montana's big die-up in the winter of 1886 was such an event. It wasn't world-wide, but every Montanan knew of it. The die-up gave them a new, significant date to mark on their calendars. Men would say reflectively, "That was the year before the big die-up," or "That happened a month after." The veterans, the people who had gone through that winter, had the authority to back their accounts. To quell opposition all a veteran had to do was to fix a bleak eye on the questioner and ask, "Were you there?" That cut the ground from under the feet of any man brash enough to argue the happening with the old-timers. Those greenhorns hadn't lost everything they owned; they hadn't seen their livestock die by the hundreds. Daily the losses mounted. Nature was a brutal scythe, each day making another swipe at the diminishing herds. Yes, a man lost material possessions, but more devastating was the loss of hope and belief.

It was believed that a Montanan could withstand anything Nature could throw at him. It was believable before that horrible, never to be forgotten winter. That winter shattered most men and bent the remaining sturdy few until they would never be quite the same again.

The beginning of this tragedy started with man's natural cupidity and the stubborn belief that Montana had an inexhaustible supply of grassland. Men literally packed Montana with new, hungry mouths. All during the preceding summer new herds were driven into Montana, many of those herds coming from as far away as Texas. The overcrowding set the stage for the following blow. These animals weren't accustomed to Montana's climate or conditions. They didn't know how to forage the year around, or how to shelter themselves. The native-born American was avid enough in his greedy search for profits, but foreign money added to that hunt and made conditions that much worse. Foreign capital poured into the country, buying up cattle to take advantage of a never-ending grass supply. Foreign money meant absentee ownership, and the owners didn't see or care what they were doing to this poor, abused land. That foreign capital arrived at a wide spread and with a growing conviction. To make more profit all that was needed was to buy new herds and crowd them onto the already overstocked Montana acres. Oh, a few wiser heads saw the folly of such a course and talked against it, but those voices were too few and too weak to be heard.

The preceding summer was accompanied by a drought, and in the searing heat, the grass shriveled instead of growing. The cattle competition grew more fierce, and the grass that was supposed to put on flesh lost in the former winter didn't materialize. Cattle slowly lost weight, and they went into the coming fall with no supply of fat. Worse, weakened cows died in the rigors of birthing calves, or produced scrawny, weakened ones. That summer's calf crop was poor. Men looked at the spindle-legged calves struggling to live and shook their heads. Still the warning wasn't strong enough to raise an alarm. Hadn't men gone through tough years before? This was a tiny leak in a bucket. It wasn't big enough to arouse concern. But if that leak wasn't stopped, it eventually drained the bucket.

So nature and man's greed set the stage for one of the greatest disasters that would ever hit this land. The first storm came in early November. It arrived with a driving force and a suddenness that literally sucked the breath out of a man's lungs. The bottom of the thermometer dropped out of sight, and the air was laden with small, white pellets that stung a man's flesh. It wasn't snow, and it wasn't sleet. No one could say for sure what it was. No one had seen anything like it before.

That storm took three days to blow out, and that was only the beginning of the misery. The country was constantly buffeted by three-barreled blows; wind, cold, and snow. Cattle drifted before the savage, driving winds. Some of the range-wise cattle found shelter in the coulees and draws and survived. The alien cattle pushed by the winds drifted until they piled up against a fence. There they perished.

Men piteously drove themselves, but their efforts did little to save the animals. It took hours to dig a single cow out of a snowbank, and all that heartbreaking effort was rewarded by seeing the exhausted animal take a few staggering steps, collapse, and die.

Ordinarily, man could expect a respite after such savage storms. But these were not ordinary times. Crippling blow after blow piled upon one after another. During one stretch of time, it snowed an inch an hour for sixteen hours, and the temperature dropped to sixty degrees below zero. If the temperature rose to zero during a day, it was considered a warming trend.

Strange tales began to circulate throughout the country. Men reported seeing unusual birds, birds never known in this country before. An old-timer finally identified them. "They're the great white owls of the Arctic," he announced. "Hell yes, I know what I'm talking about. I've seen them before." The Arctic owl was a big bird, snow-white with a rounded head and huge eyes. "When the cold drives the owls out of the Arctic," the old-timer went on, "you can believe it's cold clear to the top of the world. I'm telling you every man will wish to God he could hibernate before this winter is over."

The old-timer was too painfully right. Day after day, conditions worsened. Cattle died, and men died trying to save them. Meager supplies of hay, due to the summer's drought, ran out, and it speeded up the killing of the cattle. The chinooks with their flat, pancake-shaped clouds, signifying a warming trend, usually appeared in February. This year they didn't come. Man's last vestige of belief in a God powerful enough to change conditions vanished. The brutal cold took a new and vicious bite. More and more cattle disappeared, going down while it was snowing, not to be found until the spring thaw. There was never an accurate count of the losses, and maybe it was just as well. The figure was too staggering for an ordinary mind to assimilate.

The final report was really only a guess, but it gave magnitude to the extent of the disaster. Three hundred and sixty thousand cattle perished during that horrible winter. If a man came out with 30 per cent of his original herd, he was one of the fortunate ones. One herd of five thousand head had only one survivor, and it died shortly after the report was made. Not a fence was left in the country. In sheer desperation men cut every fence they came to, to prevent the cattle from piling up against them. Even that didn't guarantee life for these poor, starving animals. It left them to drift aimlessly until exhaustion felled them. These pitiful animals wandered into the towns, and the authorities had the problem of disposing of carcasses that finally dropped in the streets. Not a shred of anything edible was left, and that included small trees. Many a housewife, trying to beautify her yard, wailed that the cattle ate her ornamental shrubs to the ground.

There was nothing human power could do except to wait out the deadly days of the winter. One old Cree Indian, driven out of Canada by the cold, put it well when he said in his native tongue, *"Kiss-ey-oo-way's."* It was said simply but well. It meant "it blows cold."

The horrible winter broke in March, a full month later than usual. The long-awaited chinooks appeared, and the thaw started. In a couple of nights, water from the melting snow ran everywhere. The melting disclosed some of the extent of the loss. Every direction a man looked he could see just how much the winter had cost this land. The valleys and coulees were so filled with rotting carcasses that a man couldn't enter some of them because of the stench.

The winter's end left stunned, numbed minds. Few had a comprehensive plan of how to meet the future. Many would run, seeking to leave this accursed country as fast as they could. But the tough would be left, and they would try to rebuild.

Chapter One

Harl Stark walked about the buggy while he waited for Melody to come out of the house. He had gone to the house, and Ira Temple had met him at the door. Harl cussed under his breath. He had expected Temple to be at the bank. Temple had looked at him with hooded, withdrawn eyes. Harl hadn't waited for him to speak. "I'm here after Melody," he said hastily. "We arranged to go riding today."

Temple grunted, "I'll tell her," and withdrew. Those were flat, cold words, showing neither approval nor disdain.

Harl took another turn around the buggy. Temple hadn't asked him in. Harl could still feel the burn of rejection in his cheeks. Melody and Ira were as far apart as they could be. Unless a person knew them, no one would guess they were brother and sister.

Ira wasn't like his father, Harl reflected. Pike had been an openhanded man with a genuine liking for people. He had run the bank with compassion and understanding. He had built a small, struggling bank into something solid and respected. Pike gave a man every opportunity he could, and good feeling came back to him in solid waves. Ira was an entirely different matter. Ira had changed since he inherited the bank after Pike's death. Maybe the inheritance had gone to his head, Harl thought sourly. Ira acted as though he had forgotten the people on whom the bank had depended. He had tossed aside every trait that Pike had used in building the bank, and Harl thought morosely, Ira would tear down in a short time everything Pike had built.

Harl glanced again at the blank door. He wondered if Ira

had told Melody he was here. Harl wouldn't be surprised to find that he hadn't. He felt that Ira was opposed to the relationship between him and Melody. "Damn him," Harl muttered. Ira's objections would be useless. Melody had a strong will of her own. She looked up to Ira now as the head of the family, but he wasn't going to change what she thought was right. That soft, lovely appearance hid a strong streak of determination.

A chill was still in the air, and Harl stamped his boots against the ground to chase the creeping tingle. The calendar said spring, but that was only a figure on a calendar. It was really too cold for a ride, but Melody had been shut in the house for so long that Harl's offer was gratefully received.

Harl kept glancing toward the house, hoping to see the door open. His wrath mounted. Ira hadn't told Melody he was here.

His heart leaped up into his throat as he saw her come out of the front door. Even bundled up in the heavy coat, she still looked lithe and graceful. She bounded down the three steps, her head thrown back, her face flushed with pleasure at seeing him.

Harl watched her sober faced, though his eyes glistened. He was one lucky man to have a woman like this interested in him. He hadn't known Melody for a long time, but by the way he felt about her, it seemed as though it were eons. They had met at a church social last fall, and with the first meeting of their eyes something had clicked and grown steadily. Harl was twenty-five years old, but this was the first girl he had ever known who could put that flutter in his heart. Melody was a year younger than he was, and Harl considered it a small miracle that she had never married.

He seized her outstretched hands and held them as he looked into her eyes. Lord, she made a picture. The soft, gray coat went well with those laughing, brown eyes, and the russet hair showing beneath her stocking cap was a fitting crown.

She returned the pressure of his hands, her eyes still dancing. "What makes you look so solemn, Harl?"

"I thought Ira hadn't told you I was here," he replied.

That pulled a soft sigh from her. She was well aware of the ill feeling between Harl and Ira. She wished she could change that; males were stubborn creatures.

"It wasn't Ira's fault," she said. "He told me you were here. I couldn't decide what to wear."

"Forgive me, Melody," Harl apologized.

She shook her head. "Just forget it, Harl."

Harl helped her into the buggy and climbed in beside her. He unfolded the lap robe and adjusted it over her legs. "Warm enough?"

"Couldn't be more comfortable," she assured him. She was silent as he snapped the whip's popper to get the mare started.

She didn't speak until the buggy was in motion. "I wish you and Ira could be more friendly," she said wistfully.

He stiffened, trying to determine if the words were a real or fancied rebuke. "I don't feel it's my fault, Melody. Ever since Pike's funeral, Ira seems to have withdrawn further into his own world."

Melody squeezed his hand. "I know," she said in agreement. "Ira is difficult. He's so touchy these days. I can't reach him any more."

"What's on his mind?" Harl asked quietly.

"I wish I knew, Harl. At first, I thought it was the loss of his father. For so long, Ira depended on Pike to direct him in everything. Now, the reins are in his hands, and I think it's left him bewildered." She frowned thoughtfully. "You're right about him living in his own world. He's erected barriers that no one can break down. People are becoming resentful. It doesn't seem to bother him. It's almost as though he doesn't care what people think or say any more."

Harl nodded. "Pike didn't build the bank that way. I'm afraid Ira can tear it down a lot quicker than it took Pike to build it up."

"Don't you think I'm aware of that?" she cried. "I've tried to talk to him, Harl. He gets angry at the first word. If he doesn't shout at me, he storms out of the house. I've just about quit trying."

Harl felt sorry for her. It must be rough living in that big, old house with just Ira. "Can't Charley straighten him out?" Charley Duncan was the bank's teller. He had been with Pike since the day the bank opened its doors. He had a sharp head for the banking business.

"I think Charley's afraid of Ira," Melody replied and sighed. "I think he's afraid of losing his job."

That was understandable. Duncan was past seventy, and he needed the job. At his age it would be difficult to find work.

This conversation was distressing Melody, and Harl knew he should change the subject, but he had one more thing he wanted to say.

"I was surprised to find Ira at home today, Melody. I thought he'd be at the bank."

Melody shook her head. "He's got some business with Mungo Newman. I didn't dare ask him what it is. Ira was almost ready to leave when I left the house."

Harl's eyebrows shot up. Newman wasn't popular around Miles City. He had an unpredictable temper. Only last summer he had been in serious trouble with the law. He and Ben Grimes had quarreled and in the ensuing fight, Newman had shot Grimes down. Only a skilled lawyer had gotten Newman off in self-defense. Judge Hambert hadn't liked the jury's verdict, and he had lectured Newman. Harl was there the last day of the trial. Newman showed no emotion under Hambert's bitter lashing. He just stood there, stolid faced until Hambert finished.

"Don't you let me ever see you before my bench again," Hambert had finally said.

Harl turned over a dozen questions in his mind. Ira wasn't going to add to his popularity by mixing with the likes of Mungo Newman.

His next question was a personal one, but he asked it anyway. "Why do you suppose he wants to see Newman?"

Melody's face was pinched by lines of worry. "A couple of weeks ago when I was in the bank, I heard Ira tell Charley to get out Newman's account. I remember he looked over the papers and cussed."

Harl's eyes sparked with interest. It was odd that Newman would have any financial dealings with Ira's bank. Newman had a measly hundred and sixty acres, and it barely supported him and his wife. Harl was surprised that Ira would lend money on such poor property on any pretext.

"Ira say anything more?" Harl put the question as casually as he could.

Melody's forehead wrinkled. "Ira was mad because Newman was behind in his payments." Her face cleared, and she added, "He did say he was going to do something about that. I guess today's the day."

"Sounds like Ira intends to foreclose on Newman," Harl said thoughtfully.

"That could be," Melody agreed. "I know he's foreclosed on two other places recently."

"What places were those, Melody?"

"John Brinker and Ben Hammond."

Harl nodded. He knew both of those places. They were small ranches, and Harl supposed the winter's kill had knocked their owners out of business.

Melody noticed Harl's scowl, and she asked, "Does that bother you?"

Harl tried to smile. "If that's Ira's new line of thinking, it could pinch us pretty bad." His smile grew more pained. "I remember how Pike handled such things. When a man was pressed for time on a payment, Pike always extended it. A man had to be known as a thorough dead beat before Pike gobbled him up."

"All this worries you, doesn't it, Harl?"

"A lot, Melody," he confessed. "It hurts both of us." He saw that she didn't understand, and he explained, "We planned on being married this coming June, didn't we?"

Her eyes never left his face, and perhaps she sensed something bad, for a shadow of a dread filled those eyes. "What are you trying to say, Harl?"

"The winter left us in no better shape than anybody else," Harl answered soberly. "Hiram figured the final total of our loss last night. Out of eight thousand head of cattle we lost more than half."

Last summer, Harl had argued against going into debt, but that hardheaded father of his wouldn't listen. Hiram rarely listened to advice from anybody.

Harl didn't dare look at Melody as he heard an odd, little sound. It could have been a gasp or a muffled sob.

He swallowed hard, and the knuckles of the hand holding the reins stood out starkly.

"Hiram and I are going to have to ask Ira for an extension, Melody. We borrowed twelve thousand dollars last spring to buy more cattle. Hiram really believed in the prosperity of Montana cattle." He grimaced in pain as he remembered his arguments with Hiram. He had pointed out that the range was already overcrowded, but Hiram was obdurate. "You know how hardheaded Hiram is," he said with a twisted grimace.

"Oh, Harl," she cried. "All our plans—"

There was anguish in her voice, and Harl didn't want her to go on. He cut her short. "Those plans will just have to wait, Melody."

Her fingers dug into his hand. "Harl, I wouldn't mind if things were a little rough," she pleaded. "We could make it through all right."

Stubbornly, he shook his head. "That's the point, Melody. There's no guarantee we can make it through at all. I couldn't stand to drag you down into this mess." He looked squarely at her, and his eyes begged for understanding. "Damn it, Melody—" He couldn't stop the little quiver from stealing into his voice. "Do you think I want this? I've got to see Ira about an extension. The loan comes due at the end of the month. If Ira refuses to grant us more time—" He lifted a hand and let it fall, and the gesture was more eloquent than words.

"He'll listen to both of us," she said fiercely. "I'll make him."

Harl didn't shake his head, though he wanted to. Ira didn't have to listen to anybody; he owned the bank.

Melody was crying openly now. Harl's arm tightened about her shoulders. "We'll work it out," he kept repeating. They had to; they had waited so long.

She stopped crying and raised her face to his. "I know it's going to work out," she said, but her tone lacked conviction.

Harl kissed her then, trying to put enough fervor into the kiss to ease her doubts. God, how he wanted to believe her. He could take hope in the knowledge that women had better instinctive intuition than men. But this talk hadn't eased his mind. If Ira was already foreclosing on some places, a pattern could be forming in Ira's mind.

Melody shivered, and Harl asked anxiously, "Are you getting cold?"

"I guess I am, Harl." Her voice was lifeless. She tried to smile, but it was strained. "This ride didn't turn out the way we hoped, did it?"

Harl swore at himself for the things he had said. There was nothing to be gained by deepening Melody's concern. He wiped away the self-accusations. She would want to know just how things stood. She would be hurt, if he didn't confide in her.

Chapter Two

Mungo Newman paced restlessly around the poorly furnished room. Every few steps he pounded an angry fist into a meaty palm. His dull face was twisted in misery, and he looked as though every step pained him. He was a huge man, moving in a ponderous shuffle. Wrath kept boiling up in him, and he cursed the way life was. He had done his best to support his woman, and nothing had succeeded. Newman had put his best endeavors in to making this place prosper. Just when he thought he was going to make a profit the winter had wiped him out. It killed off his twenty-four head of stock and left him destitute. He had tried to save those twenty-four head, and he might have saved some of them, but those starving herds from the ranches surrounding him had broken down his fences and descended upon his pitiful stacks of hay like devouring locusts. When those alien cattle moved on, there was nothing left to feed his own stock. He had watched them starve and die, and every death was a mortal blow. He had spent the rest of the winter in a brutal struggle to survive.

Mungo Newman flexed his huge hands, and the gesture brought back the grim memory of the struggle. He had cut down every tree within view, and spent the days cutting up the wood and pulling it to the house on a sled. His endurance was awesome, and one thing drove him on: he was trying to save the woman he loved.

"Mungo, stop that pacing and look at me," a soft voice commanded.

Newman stopped and turned his head. Lord, how frail

Ruby looked. He winced at the contrast between her present appearance and the woman he had married. She was down to skin and bone, and her skin was sallow. But her eyes were still magnificent. She had known struggle all her life, and he had taken her from a home that never quite had enough to make life easy. He groaned inwardly at the lavish promises he had made her. God knew that a man never tried harder to fulfill those promises.

There had been desperate moments when he didn't think they would get through another day. He looked at her, lost in the awe of knowing she belonged to him. They had been married two years ago, and the wonder that she had seen something in him always amazed him. Each time he was near her, he went all soft inside. He couldn't remember ever being angry with her, or even impatient.

"Yes, Ruby," he rumbled.

"What's bothering you, Mungo?" At his ducking head she insisted, "I know something is wrong."

Newman's grin was twisted. "Nothing's bothering me, Ruby. Am I acting any different than usual?"

"Like a caged animal, Mungo. Don't you trust me enough to tell me what's troubling you?"

Newman walked across the room, stopping before her. "Aw, Ruby," he said in that deep voice. "I was just cussing myself for not doing better for you."

Ruby cocked her head almost birdlike. "Have I ever complained? You've done the best you could."

He shook his head in a stubborn gesture. "Not good enough, Ruby. I remember promising you I'd give you everything you ever wanted." He swept a hand about the room. "Now, look at this."

"We're together," she said softly. "I'm not asking for anything more."

He turned his head so that she couldn't see the start of tears in his eyes. "Things will get better, Ruby." Newman

wanted to curse himself again. There was another of those
hollow promises.

"All I'm asking you, Mungo, is that you stay out of trouble. I thought I'd die while you were locked up last summer.
I couldn't go through that again."

"You never will," he promised. "Ben Grimes forced me
into that argument. He said some things about you I
couldn't take."

He brushed her forehead with a kiss, straightened, and
walked to the window. The promise of spring was out there,
though there was still a bite in the air. Oh, God, he thought
despairingly. He couldn't tell her what was really troubling
him.

He heard the soft rustle of her skirt as she arose from the
chair and crossed the room to stand beside him. He put an
arm about her and pulled her close.

"Now, will you tell me what's troubling you, Mungo?"

The sigh came from the pit of his stomach. A woman had
an extra sense about trouble. He'd better tell her. She
wouldn't let him rest until he did.

"Yesterday was the fifteenth of March, Ruby."

"Yes," she said at his long pause.

"I was supposed to make a payment to the bank yesterday. I didn't have it." His dull eyes were filled with a
pleading.

"It'll work out somehow, Mungo," she insisted. "I know it
will."

He wished he could be as certain. He shook his head, and
the gesture was somehow remindful of a great wounded animal, trying to protect itself.

"I'm afraid it won't, Ruby. Mr. Temple is a hard man.
Particularly where money is involved. He'll demand his payment, or—" His voice trailed off. The prospect was too horrible to put into words.

"You mean he could take our place?" Ruby persisted.

"That's what I'm afraid of," he said heavily.

"We can start over again," she said evenly. "As long as we're together."

Newman stared out of the window not really seeing anything outside. They could lose their home—they could lose everything. He couldn't put her through the uncertainties of another start. Besides, where would that start be? He wasn't a popular man around town. He hadn't been since his trial.

"Things will turn out all right, Mungo." Conviction was in every word. "I just know it. Mr. Temple will listen to reason. He'll give us more time."

Newman couldn't bear to see that trust in her face. She didn't know Temple as he did.

He stared blindly out of the window again. He saw the rider turn off the main road that ran beside his place, and his body went rigid. He knew that familiar figure.

"Oh, God," he said hollowly. "It's him. Mr. Temple is coming."

"We'll talk to him," she said brightly. "He'll listen. Somehow, I know."

Newman watched the figure approach the house. In a moment, Temple would be beating on their door, demanding entrance. He knew what Ruby was trying to do. She was trying to bolster him, but she didn't know Temple.

Chapter Three

Ira Temple shivered as the wind blasted him afresh. He started to curse the winter for never ending, then held it. He should bless the winter; it was going to make a big man of him, a far bigger man than Pike had ever been.

He smiled malevolently. He had pretended to know grief at his father's death, but he hadn't really felt sorrow. His father had dealt harshly with him, ever since he was a child. Even after Ira reached maturity, Pike had treated him with indifference, riding roughshod over every idea he had. Why hadn't he left? Ira had pondered that question often, then with a degree of honesty admitted that he was afraid to go out on his own. Under Pike he had a job and a nebulous sense of security. Ira had cursed his reflection in the mirror, calling himself every kind of a coward he could think of. No matter how ashamed he was, no matter how his cheeks burned, he still wasn't brave enough to face the world alone. Pike gave him a job in the bank, though it never had any importance. He was little more than a bookkeeper. Even Charley Duncan could countermand anything he said. There were many times when he was livid with anger at his father's handling of some matter, but he didn't dare let Pike see a protest in his face. Pike might kick him out. The fear of that ever happening left Ira weak and trembling.

He had already resigned himself to a lifetime of drudgery and slinking about when he was handed his relief. Pike picked up a cold in the winter, and it had steadily worsened. No matter what medicine he took, he couldn't seem to shake the cold. He had gone to bed, and a week later, he was dead.

Ira's bitter smile broadened as he remembered that glorious day. Melody had wailed her head off, and Ira endured it for appearance' sake. A great feeling of release rang in his mind. He was free. He could do anything he pleased, and Pike wasn't around to block his desires.

Ira went down to the bank right after the funeral, and for three days he had done nothing except savor his new found independence. He had moved into Pike's office and, for hours at a time, had simply sat in his father's luxurious chair, enjoying his new place of prominence. He had given orders to Duncan that he didn't want to see anyone, but Duncan had dared to knock on his door.

"What do you want!" Ira had roared.

Duncan resolutely stood his ground, though he was worried. "John Brinker's here," he said. "He demands to see you, Ira. I told him you were busy, but he insists upon seeing you."

One of these days, Ira would fire Duncan for his impudence. But he would put that off, savoring the prospect. Duncan had admired Pike and often said so openly. Duncan was going to find out what his praise of Pike would cost him.

Duncan lingered in the doorway. "I think you'd better see him. He's here about his payment. It's due today."

Brinker's was one of the loans Pike had made, and Ira reconsidered. "Get me his papers."

His eyes glistened as he ran over the papers Duncan laid before him. Ira knew what Pike would have done. He would have granted an extension of time. Ira had often heard Pike brag of his policy. "This bank goes along with a customer until the last step. A bank doesn't grow over the broken bodies of its customers."

Temple leaned back in his chair. "Send Brinker in," he ordered. He knew what he was going to do. He was going to handle Brinker just the opposite of the way Pike would.

Brinker came in, a lanky man with a weather-worn face. He was nervous, and it showed in the restless closing and opening of his hands. "Howdy, Ira. I was sure sorry to hear of Pike's death."

"He'd just lived out his time," Ira said with false sorrow. "What's on your mind, John?"

"Time," Brinker said, spreading his hands eloquently. "I can't make a payment today. It's because the winter was so rough. There just ain't any way I can make it." Brinker's mouth sagged at Ira's shaking head. "You're not going to give me more time?" he spluttered.

"You read your mortgage," Temple snapped. "If you can't make a payment when it's due, the whole amount is due and collectible. It's all in the mortgage you signed."

Brinker's face turned white. "You'd take my place because I miss one payment?"

Temple leaned back in his chair. "You catch on quick," he said coldly. "That's the way it lies."

Brinker cursed him with every oath at his command.

"That doesn't change anything," Temple said in clipped tones.

"One of these days, somebody's going to blow your head off," Brinker said furiously. "By God, I'm tempted to do it myself."

"You'd hang for it," Temple said frozenly. "Duncan," he bellowed. "Mr. Brinker's finished his business."

He had watched a broken man shuffle out of his office. This was power, and he was drunk on the taste. He had discovered a startling fact; he could make people look up to him, he could make them fearful. He didn't know what he was going to do with the Brinker place, but he'd think of something.

He had gone to Toucey Stevens, his lawyer, and had drawn up the eviction papers. He then handed the eviction notice to Quincy Rader and enjoyed the frown spreading across Rader's face as he read them.

"This isn't going to make you very popular, Ira."

"That's my business," Temple snapped. "As sheriff you have to enforce those papers."

Rader stared at Temple with blank eyes. "I wish to God I thought you knew what you're doing. Pike wouldn't have done this."

"Pike's dead," Temple said matter-of-factly. "You're dealing with me."

He had looked back as he left the office. Rader sat there, staring at the eviction notice.

Temple foreclosed on Ben Hammond two weeks later. He had gone through the same scene he had gone through with Brinker. He had withstood Hammond's cursing without flinching. Words couldn't hurt a man. It was the power a man held that he could use on another man that counted.

He spent three days thinking about the Brinker and Hammond places. Then the idea had blasted through his head like a bolt of lightning. Land was selling poorly in Montana right now, but that wouldn't last forever. One of these days when things returned to normal, prices would soar. If a man held enough of that land, he would become one of the greatest powers in Montana. Ira Temple could become one of the greatest powers in Montana. Hiram Stark, he thought, clenching his fist so hard that it hurt. Stark owned twelve thousand acres of prime Montana land, and he owed a payment by the end of the March. If Temple could get his hands on Stark's ranch, he would be well on the way to becoming one of the largest landholders in the state.

The magnitude of his plan flushed his face and made his heart pound. He could be grateful to Pike for one thing; for loaning out so much money. After his foreclosure on Stark, there would be others.

He made a thorough examination of all the papers the bank held. Every one had that same damning clause; miss a payment and lose the land. Temple didn't know why Pike had insisted on that clause. He had never used it to his advantage.

Temple's pulses were racing as he looked at the future. After Stark, there would be others. He could wind up the wealthiest and most powerful man in Montana.

It all depended on whether or not Stark could make his payment. Temple thought the answer to that was negative. Stark wouldn't be in any better shape than Brinker and Hammond. But this foreclosure had to be handled more carefully than the other two. Stark was known for his irascible temper, and it could explode in Temple's face.

Temple stood and paced around his desk. Did he want to face Stark? The answer to that was a definite yes. He had the law on his side. Stark might rave and storm, but outside of that, what could he do?

He could blow your head off as Brinker had suggested, a timorous voice in Temple's head said.

Just the thought of violence put a hard knot in Temple's throat and brought out the sweat on his forehead. The possibility wasn't beyond Stark's temper. Suppose the scene in his office blew up in his face. Sweat ran harder on his face. How was he going to stop Stark from carrying it to those extremes? He needed protection, somebody to stop Stark from carrying out his wrath.

Temple's eyes gleamed, and he walked back to his desk and sank limply into his chair. There was the crux of his plan. He had to get Stark out of his office without endangering himself.

His fingers drummed as he turned his plan over and over. If he had somebody in the office with him, somebody big and rough enough to stop Stark in his tracks, there would be no violence. The sweating stopped, and he pounded the desk with his fist. A guard, something like a security guard was the answer. Somebody with a reputation who wouldn't care how angry Stark became.

A sharp breath whistled through Temple's lips. The an-

swer was right before his eyes, and he hadn't seen it. On his
desk was the paper on Mungo Newman's place. Temple
knew he was going to have to foreclose on Newman's place,
but that little, piddling piece of land had no great interest to
him. But if he could tie Newman to him with the offer of a
job, Newman's gratitude would be unending. He would go
to any lengths to protect the man who gave him security.

"There it is," Temple exclaimed aloud. He had a trip to
make to the blacksmith's, then he would ride out and see
Newman.

Color returned to his face, and his hands were steady
again. Nothing could stop him from becoming one of the
biggest men in Montana.

He put on a sheepskin coat and set his hat on his head. He
walked out of his office and passed Duncan's cage. "Charley, I have to go out. Something I have to attend to."

Worry clouded Duncan's tired, old eyes. "Something I
could do for you, Mr. Temple?"

Temple snorted at the question. This old man didn't have
the heart this job would take. He walked on by the cage
without answering.

Chapter Four

Old man Jenkins brought Temple's horse to him. "Going out to kick somebody else off, Ira?" Jenkins had an obscene sense of humor, and he cackled, displaying toothless gums.

"None of your damned business," Temple growled. He jerked the reins from Jenkins' hands and swung up into the saddle.

"Keep on the way you're going," Jenkins called after him, "and you'll find people colder than a witch's heart." He cackled again, highly pleased with his wit.

"Old fool," Temple fumed as he rode out of the stable. Where in the hell had Jenkins gotten his information? That wasn't too hard to answer. Brinker and Hammond had probably cussed him out all over town. Jenkins, upon seeing him riding out, had just made a shrewd conjecture. It didn't matter. Nothing was going to change him from the course he had picked.

Temple muttered against the bite in the air and burrowed deeper into his sheepskin. What mood would he find Newman in? Temple thought about that all the way to Newman's place.

Temple had never seen a place that screamed of poverty more than this one did. He didn't see a single head of any kind of livestock, not even a dog or cat, and the house was a disreputable place for humans to live. Newman wasn't the best of handymen. None of the attempted repairs fitted or matched, and the bare lumber was in stark contrast to the once-painted house. Several windows had been broken out. On some, Newman had tried to cover the gaps with oiled paper. If it was only a small pane, he had stuffed rags into the hole.

Temple swung down heavily, his face set in cold disdain. There was no doubt that Newman was barely getting by. He wouldn't have to offer Newman much to have him jump at the prospect of a job.

Temple was putting on too much weight, and just the short walk to the front door made him wheeze. Before he knocked, he pulled out the badge he had had made at the blacksmith's. It was a crude six-pointed star, hammered out of a thick piece of tin. Lykens had lettered "Security Guard" across the badge. It wasn't a very appealing piece of work, but Temple had been in such a hurry that he had accepted it. At least, Sheriff Rader didn't know anything about his idea. Rader would raise hell at such a suggestion. He might even forbid Temple to use this scheme. Temple's lips twisted in a mirthless grin. He didn't give a damn what Rader thought. In a short time, he would know whether or not the idea was practical.

Temple dropped the badge back into his sheepskin pocket as he reached the door. All the way here he had been aware he was under observation. He had seen a slight stir in the ragged green blind in a front window.

Maybe Newman wouldn't let him in. He grunted at the absurdity of the thought. Newman didn't dare refuse him anything.

He raised a hand and knocked sharply.

Temple waited for what seemed an inordinate amount of time. He knocked again and said, "Mungo, I know you're in there. I saw the window shade lift and fall. You'd better open this door."

The door opened, and Newman's huge dull face was framed in the opening. "I was sitting down, Mr. Temple. I was a little slow getting up. Come in, come in."

A frail woman stood beside him. It didn't look as though Newman made enough to keep her well fed.

"Mr. Temple," Newman said. "This is Ruby. My wife!"

Temple grunted his acknowledgment and pushed on by the couple.

He crossed to the only sturdy-looking chair in the room and gingerly lowered his bulk into it.

"I know why you're here, Mr. Temple," Newman babbled on.

"Do you?" Temple asked with cruel enjoyment. "Then suppose you tell me."

A choking spell cut off Newman's words. He coughed until his eyes bulged. When he could speak again, he asked, "Would you like a cup of coffee, Mr. Temple?"

A wave of Temple's hand dismissed that idea. "I'm here on business, Mungo."

That sounded like a stifled groan coming from Newman. "I know it's about that payment, Mr. Temple. I couldn't get in yesterday."

Temple snorted in disbelief. "Did you expect to come in today?"

Newman pulled at his fingers, his face a mask of distress. "I guess not," he managed to get out and fell silent.

Ruby stepped forward. "The truth is that we haven't the payment, Mr. Temple. But we'll have it. All we need is a little more time."

"Sure you do," Temple said and smiled.

Ruby's face turned white and she gasped. That smile and the words had to be pure mockery. Her hand went to her breast, and she breathed hard. "I mean it, Mr. Temple. All we need—"

Another wave of his hand cut her short. "I know. Time. That's what I'm here to talk about. How would you like a job in my bank, Mungo? As long as you work for me, we could forget about the payment."

Newman's face turned alternately white and red as he struggled to understand what Temple was saying. A dawning hope illuminated his face. "But I never worked in a bank before, Mr. Temple." He looked down at his hands, engrossed in pulling at the misshapen knuckles. "I'm not very good with figures."

"The job wouldn't be with figures," Temple said softly. "I need a guard to protect the bank's property." He pulled the crude badge from his pocket and handed it to Newman.

Newman studied it carefully, turning it over and over. "What would I do?"

Lord, Temple thought impatiently. This man couldn't get anything through his head. "You would stand guard. If any of the customers get belligerent, you'd stop them."

Newman nodded his understanding. "I'd protect you?"

"You've got it," Temple said heartily. "You'd be surprised how rough a disgruntled man can get over money matters."

Newman nodded solemnly. "I can just bet." He knew from his own case just how frantic a man could become. "You don't need to worry any more."

Temple kept the curl out of his lip. There had never been any real worry in him since the start. Everything was working out the way he hoped. Should he tell Newman about Stark now, or wait a few days? He decided upon the latter. He had some time until the end of the week.

He stood and said brusquely, "Then I can look for you tomorrow?"

"I'll be there," Newman said joyously. "Will it be all right to wear my gun in the bank?"

"I'm hiring you as a guard," Temple said in disgust. "You wouldn't do much good without your gun, would you?" He managed a stiff smile. It took a lot of pounding to get an idea into Newman's head. He pondered upon how much money to offer Newman and decided on ten dollars a week. There was no sense squandering money. Besides, Newman wouldn't be at the bank long.

"I'm offering you ten dollars a week, Mungo. Does that sound all right to you?"

Temple saw Newman and Ruby exchange looks, looks of

incredible joy. That answered his question. "I'll expect you in the morning," he said and moved toward the door.

"I won't disappoint you," Newman said. His lips trembled so much he could scarcely speak.

I don't think you will, Temple thought bleakly. He nodded to the couple and closed the door behind him. Lord, why was he shaking so? His plan was going just as he had plotted it. Tomorrow he would tell Newman the real reason he had hired him. He would alert him to keep his eyes open for Hiram Stark. A disquieting thought put a pall over his expectations. What if Hiram came in to make his payment? Then all of Temple's planning would be for naught.

No, he thought savagely, dismissing the unhappy thought. Stark would be no different from anybody else. He was in the same boat, the boat that had wrecked every Montana rancher's dreams.

Chapter Five

Temple restlessly paced his office. It was a few minutes after nine, and Newman hadn't arrived. Temple snorted at a thought. Maybe Newman didn't know the hour the bank opened. His face contorted. He was relying so much on Newman's part in this. Had Newman thought it over and decided to withdraw? No, he thought violently. This was Newman's only way to pull himself out of a hole. He wouldn't pass up this chance.

His head snapped around at a knock on his door. That would be Duncan. Duncan didn't dare enter this office without asking permission.

Temple strode to the door and flung it open. "What is it?" he snapped.

Duncan stared stolid faced at him, though a muscle at the corner of his mouth twitched. Duncan was uneasy around Temple, though he had too much pride to ever admit or show it. Ever since Temple had taken over the reins of the bank, Duncan hadn't been able to figure out which direction Temple was going. Duncan had never made a great deal of money, but he had lived fairly comfortably while Pike ran this bank. The big trouble was that he hadn't saved enough money so that he could retire. He had to keep on working, and his sense of security was gone. He never knew what that unpredictable temper of Ira's would do.

"Someone out here to see you, sir," he said huskily.

"Who is it?"

"It's Mungo Newman. I had to be sure you wanted to see him before I let him in."

"I do," Temple barked. "Show him in." He didn't miss the start of surprise that washed across Duncan's face. Newman must be pretty seedy-looking. "Do I have to tell you again?"

"No, sir," Duncan said hastily and withdrew.

Temple reseated himself at his desk while he waited for Newman to appear. A thought flashed across his mind: he could dismiss Newman and let everything stop where it was. Then he discarded the idea. There could be an element of danger in his scheme, but there was always danger when a man set his sights on higher goals.

Newman dwarfed the office. He looked even bigger than he had in his own house. Temple noted sardonically that Newman had tried to improve his appearance. Newman couldn't do much about the sheepskin. It was well worn around the elbows, and old age had turned it black, particularly around the collar. But his shirt was freshly washed and ironed, and the jeans though old were carefully patched. He had tried to polish his boots, but there wasn't enough polish to disguise the scuffs and runover heels. He was following Temple's instructions. His old, black gun was prominent on his hip.

"Sit down, Mungo. Sit down." Temple tried to put warmth in his voice. "All ready to work at your new job?"

Newman sat down, but he wasn't comfortable. He sat on the chair's edge, and he looked as though he would bound to his feet at any instant. Those cowlike eyes fired with a new enthusiasm. "You don't know what you've done for Ruby and me," he rumbled. "You gave us hope. It's been a long time since I've worked. I couldn't find a job anywhere." He raised his hands and let them fall helplessly. "Ruby and me talked most of the night about it. We were still talking about it this morning. That's what made me a little late."

Temple waved a hand, dismissing the admission of guilt. "No matter. You're here now."

"You'll have to tell me what you want," Newman said apologetically. "Just tell me, and it'll be done."

"I'm sure it will be," Temple responded. "There won't be much to do. Maybe the days will seem dreary to you. But I want you to keep alert. Watch every customer. If one of them shows unhappiness or anger, I want you to cut him short. Don't worry. I'll back every move you think it is necessary to make."

Newman's eyes were filled with doglike devotion. "I sure appreciate that, Mr. Temple." Curiosity overcame him, and he asked, "Does some particular customer bother you?"

"Not right now," Temple answered somberly. "But I'm afraid it could happen. I'm expecting Hiram Stark by the end of the month. Do you know him?"

"I know him," Newman said flatly. "I ain't got much use for him. He's the one who ordered my fences cut when his cattle piled up against them. Those damned cattle swept over my place, devouring every bit of hay I had. Left me nothing to feed my own stock. All I could do was stand by and watch my own stock starve to death."

"That's horrible." Temple's face showed the proper concern. Inside, he was exultant. This couldn't be set up any better, if he had hand-picked the pieces. Newman already knew an animosity toward Stark. It wouldn't be hard to work him up into a rage.

"I saw a long time ago I couldn't do anything about it," Newman said flatly.

"Maybe you can," Temple said smoothly. "I don't mind admitting that Stark worries me. You know his temper."

"He won't show any of it in here as long as I'm around," Newman announced. "I won't even let him into your office, if you say so."

Temple sadly shook his head. "I'm afraid I'll have to talk to him. I'm hoping he'll listen to reason." He spread his hands eloquently on his desk. "I'm not a violent man, but

I'm afraid of Stark's temper. I don't know what I would do, if Stark loses his head."

"Don't worry any more about it," Newman advised. "When Stark comes in, I'll follow him into your office. If he gets out of hand, I'll stop him."

"You don't know how much that eases my mind," Temple said. He was tired of listening to this simple man. "Why don't you go out and have Duncan show you around. I'll call you, if I need you."

Newman burnished the crude badge with his shirt cuff. "I'll come arunning."

He stood and shuffled out of the office. Temple watched contemptuously. That poor, dumb ox. Everything had fitted neatly into place. Now, all he had to do was wait for Hiram Stark to show.

A few things still bothered Temple. Quincy Rader might have some hard questions when he heard that Newman was working at the bank. Temple bristled defensively. This was his business; he could hire anybody he wanted. He didn't give a damn how much Rader might rant and rave.

He picked up a cigar and leaning back, put his feet up on the desk. He was on his way to being one of the biggest men in Montana. All he had to do was to wait out the time until Stark showed up in the office. At the merest suggestion of foreclosure, Stark's famous temper would take over. Temple shivered at the thought of how that temper could explode into violence. He pulled deeply on his cigar to quiet his trembling nerves. Wasn't that why he had hired Newman: to stop any violence from touching him?

Chapter Six

Duncan's eyes were failing, but they weren't bad enough for him not to notice the shadow that fell across his ledger. The size of the shadow told him who it was. Some streak of obstinacy kept Duncan from acknowledging Newman's presence. He hadn't liked the man when he first saw him; his liking hadn't grown any better while he showed Newman about the bank.

Newman tentatively cleared his throat, and Duncan stubbornly kept his eyes fixed on the ledger. He was nearing his seventieth year, and his hands were getting shaky. Things had certainly changed since Pike's death. The hiring of this big hulk Newman was an indication of the trend, and from what Duncan could determine it was all bad.

He snorted derisively. Imagine Ira hiring a bank guard. Pike had never needed one, and Duncan could say positively that they didn't need one now. Ira was getting fancy. Pike must be turning over in his grave. No wonder Ira had aroused Pike's anger so often. Ira had a habit of doing damned fool things.

Newman cleared his throat and said softly, "Pardon me, but—"

"I ain't got any time to talk," Duncan said petulantly. "Go find somebody else to talk." Oh, God, if only he had saved enough money so that he could quit now. That was an impossible dream. He scarcely made enough money to live on and he was helping support a sister. Saving anything after buying the necessities was out of the question.

He slammed the ledger shut and rudely turned his back on the waiting man. Maybe that could get him in hot water. Ira might raise hell if he heard about it. Duncan wondered if Newman was the kind of a man who ran to Ira with tales. If so, Duncan didn't give a damn. He might be fired, but there ought to be other banks that needed an experienced teller.

He looked back over his shoulder as he got the day's money from the safe. Newman still stood there, looking perplexed.

"Let him chew on that," Duncan growled to himself. He came back and distributed the day's supply of cash in his cash drawer. He was ready for another day's work. This one would be no different from all the other days.

Newman was still there when Duncan returned to his cage. He cleared his throat, then asked hesitantly, "Please, Mr. Duncan. Can I talk to you?"

"Can't you see I'm busy?" Duncan growled. "I ain't got an easy job like you. I've got more to do than to stand around all day long."

That's all he'd seen Newman do in the past week. He had no idea what Ira paid him, but by any standards, it was too much. Duncan hadn't hired this stupid ox; it wasn't up to him to soothe his feathers.

Duncan didn't look up as he heard the scrape of Newman's boots. Finally, Newman turned and shuffled to the front wall near the door and resumed his usual position.

Duncan's anger was still with him. It was like Ira to throw money away when he hadn't offered Duncan the smallest raise.

Johnson, the feed store man, came into the bank, and Duncan noticed him turn his head to look at Newman as he passed him.

Johnson came up to the cage, pulling a passbook and

some bills from his pocket. "Selby paid me a long overdue bill, Charley. Thought I'd better get it into the bank."

"Smart," Duncan approved. "You're one of the lucky ones. Being able to make a deposit."

Johnson looked sharply at Duncan to see if that was sarcasm, then decided none was intended. "I sure am," he agreed, his usual affability returning. "Things are getting pretty hairy, Charley. I've got a hunch a man's going to be scraping pretty hard before things straighten out."

"God's truth," Duncan said solemnly. He wished he had a little money to pay some of the bills he owed.

Johnson was in a talkative mood. "Ira seems to be doing pretty well. Hiring new help like that." He jerked his head in Newman's direction. "Kind of a fancy title, ain't it? Security guard." He snorted in derision. "What does he do to earn his pay?"

Duncan was tempted to say, "Damned if I know. I haven't seen him do anything." He wisely held his tongue. Any remark might get back to Ira, and Duncan knew the wrath that would arouse. "Ask Mr. Temple, if you want to know."

Johnson shrugged. "Not that important. Just curious." He picked up his passbook, inspected the fresh entry, and nodded with satisfaction.

"See you again, Charley."

"Sure," Duncan replied grumpily. He hoped no more customers came in all day. He didn't feel like either work or talk.

He returned to his open inspection of Newman. What was it going to take to make Newman move? Duncan shook his head. He sure didn't know.

He bent over his ledger and spewed out his resentment of Ira Temple again. Ira was a tightfisted man with a nickel when it came to a man who had worked for his family for a long string of years. But he didn't hesitate to go out and hire a worthless man like Newman. Ira wouldn't get a nickel's

worth of work out of him. Duncan chuckled to himself in
sour humor. Ira would find that out. The malevolent
thought lifted Duncan's spirits a little. He could get through
the rest of the day.

Chapter Seven

Harl Stark's eyes kept shifting about the country. His rest-
lessness spoke of his inner turmoil. He kept thinking of the
distress in Melody's eyes, and he couldn't do a damned
thing to remove it. After that horrible winter, he could see
no prospects of anything better. It would take another year
of drudgery just to scrape through.

Harl was seeing this country in an entirely new light. His
face was set in sober lines as he thought back over the past
few months. Sure, he knew a gratitude for having survived
the winter. But the resentment far outweighed the gratitude. A man shouldn't be put through a winter like that. He
had been born in Montana, and all of his twenty-five years
were spent here. He thought he knew this country as well as
anybody his age could know it, but last winter had jolted
him into a new awareness. He would never look again at
this country with the same easy acceptance. Even during
the ordinary times, there had been stretches of bad weather,
but its severity was usually dulled after a few days. The last
winter was so brutally cold that he never felt warm, even
sitting near a roaring fire. The damned snow fell day after
day until Harl thought he would go crazy watching it pile
up. Some of the old-timers spoke knowingly of the killer
winter, saying it was a freak. Once a man went through one
such winter, he would never have to go through another in
his lifetime.

Harl didn't believe that. He knew that hope was the basis
of the statement. It had happened once, and it was possible
for it to happen again. He cursed the memory of that winter

deep in his heart. Once in a lifetime was more than enough.

His eyes made another sweep of the country. All this beloved land once so well known to him was now an alien country. Never again would he feel so free and sure of himself. From now on, he would keep an apprehensive eye on the skies, waiting for the beginning of another blow.

Harl glanced at the rider accompanying him. Hiram Stark rode in his usual silence, his thoughts hidden behind that granitelike facade. The winter had touched Harl's father just as it had touched every life. Hiram was never a loquacious man, but now it was as though he had forgotten how to speak.

There was censure in Harl's eyes as he looked at his father. Hiram was a hard man to get close to. He was a man of varied moods, and Harl was never certain what would come next. His father frequently lost his temper, and nobody could talk him out of his foul turn of disposition. All one could do was wait until that bad streak wore thin and eventually vanished. Hiram never apologized to anybody for displaying his bad side.

Harl sighed at the onslaught of heavy thoughts. He couldn't say he loved his father. Too many years of obstinate, bad temper had thoroughly trampled his affection. All Harl could say was that he felt respect. Maybe when he grew much older, that respect would grow into something warmer, though he doubted that. It was almost as though Hiram were fearful of affection and did everything in his power to keep it at arm's length. Right now, Harl guessed he would have to settle for respect.

His mother had told him years ago he was named after his grandfather. Hiram said he didn't want a second Hiram in the family. Harl remembered Grandfather Harl Stark as a tough, old coot with laughter constantly bubbling up to his lips. He didn't have the temper that his son had. Harl remembered seeing his grandfather only twice in a number of years. Hiram just hoped young Harl could wear the name as

well as old Harl had. Father and son weren't cast in the
same mold, for Harl was a good three inches taller, and his
eyes were gray instead of blue. He was built more on the
lines of a fencing sword where Hiram had the bluntness and
thickness of a cavalry saber. One thing they did have in
common was determination. Once they took hold of a problem, they never let go until the problem was whipped to
their satisfaction or they dropped from sheer exhaustion.

Hiram suddenly broke into that familiar, hacking cough,
and it racked him as severely as though somebody had
beaten him on the back.

"Goddamned thing," he gasped when the paroxysm
finally released him. "Don't think I'll never get rid of it."

That was typical of Hiram. He could complain and cuss
this cold, but he wouldn't do anything concrete to whip it.
Harl was concerned about that cold hanging on, and that
concern annoyed him. That was typical of Hiram, to cuss
and complain without trying to get professional help. The
cold had hit Hiram right after the beginning of winter, and
it had hung on with a wolf-like ferocity. In all fairness, he
had tried every home remedy Addie knew or had heard of,
but he had never sought a doctor's help.

"You better see Doctor Neal when we get in town," Harl
advised coldly.

Hiram snorted his derision. "Won't do a damned bit of
good. He'll load me up with his fancy cures that won't accomplish a damned thing except run up my bill."

He reached into a hip pocket, pulled out a fresh ban-
danna, gripped the end of his nose, and blew vigorously. He
carefully folded the handkerchief, muttering caustically as
he thrust it into a sheepskin pocket. "Getting so a man can
hardly keep a fresh handkerchief on him," he said wrathfully.

Harl wanted to stop Hiram from going into another ti-
rade. "Didn't you bring enough handkerchiefs with you?"

"You think I can't take care of myself?" Hiram demanded.

Harl sighed. Hiram was in a quarrelsome mood today. Harl kept his tone mild. "I was just reminding you."

"You reminded me," Hiram said stiffly.

Something was bothering Hiram bad, and Harl could guess at what it was. Last winter was a continuation of bad news that slammed into them every way they turned. Hiram must have gotten more bad news.

Harl kept his attention on the country. When Hiram wanted him to know what was bothering him, he would tell him.

Spring had finally arrived. Harl couldn't say it had been slow in coming. It was only the waiting for its arrival that seemed so long drawn out. Most of the snow was gone, only a white covering remaining on the higher elevations. Spring had come with a rush after it had cruelly wracked everyone by its tardiness. It wasn't just imagination. A faint patina of green was beginning to steal over the ground, and tree buds were swelling, bursting with new life. At this rate, in less than a week's time the trees would be putting on a fresh green coat. Harl looked at the Square Buttes and the Highwoods rising up to their right. The snow covering was still on them, but it was receding rapidly. A man could go to sleep at night, wake up in the morning, and see how much the thawing had gained. It wasn't just a yearning hope; the thawing was actually happening. Due south was Judith Gap, leading to the Judith Mountains. To the left of the gap was the long, snowcapped ridge of the Little Snowies. Far to the northeast, the hazy, blue forms of the Bearpaw Mountains rose across the Missouri River. They were all friendly sights, but Harl looked at them with an unforgiving eye. They hadn't been friendly last winter. He wondered if he could ever regain the old feeling he once had for this country.

He unbuttoned his sheepskin and let it hang open. Hiram started to do the same, and Harl stopped him. "You want to make that cold worse?"

"How long do I have to nurse this damned thing?" Hiram grumbled. "All summer?"

"As long as it takes," Harl said flatly. He wasn't arguing, he was merely stating an inescapable fact. Oh, he sympathized with Hiram, but sympathy wasn't going to do him any good right now.

Hiram cursed the cold with a sudden, bitter burst of oaths.

"Never heard of a man curing a cold that way," Harl said practically. He wanted to ride into Miles City with a reasonable degree of calmness. Hiram's losing his head wasn't going to gain him a thing.

"This is just another damned echo," Hiram fumed.

"What's that mean?" Harl asked absently. His thoughts were preoccupied with the coming day's business, and he wasn't sure he heard Hiram right.

"This cold," Hiram explained. "It's an echo of the winter. When something that severe happens, you can expect hundreds of echoes."

Harl wasn't quite sure just what Hiram was trying to say. "Do you mean that everything bad that happens from now on can be attributed to the winter?"

Hiram nodded seriously. "When something that big happens, it sets up little ripples that keep smashing into people." He paused, trying to express a clearer meaning. "It's like you throw a stone into a pool of water. A lot of circles form where the stone went in. Those circles keep getting bigger and bigger. They finally fade out, but they keep coming for a long time. That winter was the stone smashing into our lives."

Harl grinned, amused. He started to scoff, then held it. Maybe Hiram had something there after all. It could be a convenient thing at that. If anything bad happened to you, blame it on an echo.

A sudden shift in the wind carried a rank, offensive odor to Harl, and his nose wrinkled in disgust.

Hiram caught it at the same time, and resentment flooded his face. It wasn't a new smell. With the thawing, frozen animals were beginning to rot. A man could hardly ride any place without that smell of death assailing him. Dead cattle were strewed all over this country. Nothing could be done about the carcasses. All man could do was to wait helplessly until nature and the predators cleaned up the rotting bodies.

Harl was afraid Hiram would point out another echo, and he said sharply, "You've made your point. Don't pound on it any more."

Hiram was in a cantankerous mood, and he ignored Harl's admonishment. "Going to be a good season for the damned wolves and coyotes. Plenty of meat lying around without them hardly having to move to get at it."

Hiram was determined to bring up all the unpleasant things he could.

"Don't forget about the magpies," Harl pointed out dryly.

"I hate those things about as much as I do all the other varmints," Hiram said passionately. "The first thing those foul things do is to go after a helpless animal's eyes."

Hiram was like a cheap clock wound too tightly. If he kept on in this vein, he was going to shatter into pieces.

Harl shook his head. Hiram was going to have his way. Harl might as well let him get it out of his system. "Now, what are you driving at?" he asked in resignation.

"Things like the wolves and magpies make you wonder if there's really anything like a Divine Being who looks after you. How can we help but question that when everything in this damned world is so set against us?"

"You better hadn't let Ma hear you say that," Harl advised.

Hiram winced at the thought of the wrath such heresy would arouse in Addie. She would rip off his hide. "I don't care," he said stubbornly. "Nobody can tell me a God sits up there, looking after me."

Harl shrugged. The question was too big for him even to

talk about. "I don't know, Pa," he said, hoping the subject
would drop there.

Hiram wasn't that easily turned aside. "You know
damned well there isn't," he said positively. "Isn't that God
supposed to be powerful enough to control everything that
touches a man's life?"

Harl sighed. Hiram couldn't be shut off, not until he said
what was on his mind. "That's what the preachers say," he
admitted cautiously.

"Hah!" Hiram exploded. "If you believe what the
preachers say, then you think there's a God protecting you
from everything bad. If there is such a thing, then you've
got to believe He sent all the bad weather last winter. Look
at how much suffering and death it caused man and animal.
Can you believe in a God like that?"

"It's damned hard to believe," Harl said in that same cautious tone. His eyes were bleak as he remembered all the
privation and suffering he had seen last winter. A man's
stomach was almost ripped out of him every time he saw another animal literally starving or freezing to death. It was
natural to feel compassion for those suffering animals. If
there was a higher power, certainly man expected a greater
compassion from Him.

"Damn it, Hiram," he said plaintively. "The whole thing's
too much for me to figure out."

Hiram thought he sensed a weakening in Harl's argument,
for his voice strengthened. "Would you like to think that a
God like that was holding back another winter like the last
one to hit us with in another few years?"

"God forbid." The words tore out of Harl's mouth before
he realized what he was saying. It was further proof that
even subconsciously a man believed in a strong power that
guarded him. It was difficult to speak more than a few
words without making some reference to that power.

"So you see it too," Hiram continued. "There just ain't
anything up there that protects a man. Whatever protection

he gets, he makes for himself. I know damned well I sure ain't worshipping a God who can do that to me."

Harl looked speculatively at him. This was the first time he had ever heard Hiram speak out like this. He must have been carrying this load on his mind for a long time, and the burden had become too great to bear any longer. Maybe last winter had honed his tongue until he could no longer control it.

"I only know one thing," Harl said with conviction. "It's too much for any man to say he's right, or another to say he's wrong. There's nothing either of them can do to change a thing."

Hiram looked as though he were suddenly spent. "You're right about one thing. It sure doesn't do any good to argue about whether or not there is a God." He rode several hundred yards in silence. "Don't burden your mind with it, Harl."

Harl grinned sardonically at him. That was so typical of Hiram. He snorted and stomped around until he got everybody thoroughly riled up, then placidly said, "Forget it." Harl stared straight ahead. Hiram's words were still ringing in his mind. He would drive himself plumb crazy trying to figure out what it was all about. Men had been arguing about God since they found the ability to talk, and no man had been able to prove his contention one way or the other.

Hiram grinned sheepishly. "Guess I was just trying to find something to blame for all the misery we've known."

"You can't stop thinking about the misery," Harl said darkly. "A lot of outfits have gone under, or are going to. What are the people of Montana going to do, Pa?"

Hiram's jaw jutted forward, and he looked twenty years younger. "Why, they'll pick themselves up and go on."

Harl started to speak, and Hiram cut him short. "Don't try to tell me I'm wrong. I know a lot of men will pull out, running for a more desirable climate. But plenty will stay and start building anew."

The weighing look returned to Harl's face. "I just hope they've learned enough not to overload the range again," Harl said passionately.

Hiram's face darkened. "That another jab at me, Harl?" He shook his head, cutting off Harl's answer. "I know I was one of the leaders in that damn-fool movement. I insisted on bringing in more cattle. I remember how mad you made me, telling me to go slower. I only had one thing in mind: get bigger and bigger. I overloaded the range with no proper planning of how to take care of the animals I had. I learned a bitter lesson. I'll never overload again."

Some of the judging left Harl's eyes. In all the years he had known Hiram, Harl had never heard him admit a mistake. As bad as the winter had been, it was almost worth going through it, if it made Hiram change his stubborn thinking. This was the first reasonable meeting of minds he had ever known with his father. As long as they were talking this openly, he might as well ask the question that loomed so frighteningly in his mind.

"Can we pull through, Pa?" he asked quietly. Oh, he knew the final tally. Out of eight thousand head of cattle, they had less than half that number remaining. Rebuilding would be a rough hill to climb.

"What makes you ask that, Harl?"

The evasiveness in Hiram's voice tightened Harl's face. Goddamn it! He had worked his butt off on the Bow Gun. He had a right to know how bad their situation really was.

The set of Harl's face made Hiram sigh. "It depends on several things, Harl. I looked at the remaining cattle yesterday. We can forget about a spring roundup. We'll probably lose some more head. Some of the cows are too weak to make it. The ones who do will have a poor calf crop. There won't be enough to think of selling any." He fell silent, staring straight ahead.

"What else does our getting through depend on, Pa?" Harl asked, waiting for his father to admit the worst.

Hiram's face looked as though it were ravaged by all the worries a man could know. He took so long in answering that Harl's temper was beginning to rise.

"Pa," he said in a clipped tone.

Hiram's sigh was an admission of defeat. "You've got every right to know, son. I didn't ask you to ride into town with me to pick up supplies. This is the roughest spot I've ever known."

A dread was beginning to steal through Harl's body, making him rigid. "Go on, Pa," he said in that same unforgiving tone.

"It's that loan I made from Pike. Twelve thousand dollars with the Bow Gun as collateral. The first payment is due today. And I haven't got it."

Harl sorted through his addled thoughts. "And Pike died. It leaves Ira in charge. We won't even be dealing with the same man."

"That's about it, Harl," Hiram admitted in a low voice.

For a blind moment, Harl wanted to smash his father in the face. But that would accomplish nothing. He drew a deep breath, and the words came out calmly enough. "Is it going to wipe us out, Pa?"

From somewhere Hiram found the strength to reply, "Hell no. It might cripple us, but it won't bring us down."

Harl glared at him. He couldn't see why this disaster wasn't the finishing blow. "The payment is supposed to be made today?"

"I said so, didn't I?" Hiram answered petulantly.

"What's the use of riding in to see Ira, if we can't make the payment?"

Hiram straightened in his saddle. "Pike would have given us an extension."

Harl groaned. Dear God! Would he ever get anything through his father's stubborn head? "We're not dealing with Pike," he said savagely.

"I'll make Ira listen to reason," Hiram said. "By God, I'll make him."

Harl glanced coldly at the gun on Hiram's hip. "With that?" Hiram had carried it for twenty years. Now, it was mainly a habit. It had been a long time since he had needed a gun.

"He'll listen," Hiram repeated stubbornly. He stole a covert glance at Harl. "You sore at me, son?"

"Shouldn't I be?"

"Every right in the world," Hiram answered. "It was my hardheadedness that put us so deep in a hole. You begged me not to buy those cattle." Hiram worked himself up to the task of self-flogging. "I wouldn't listen. I was too smart, too big for anything to ever happen to me. If I had listened to you, we'd had fewer cattle to bring through, more hay to feed what we had, and the cattle would have come through better."

"It's kind of late to be looking at facts," Harl said coldly.

Hiram looked straight ahead. His eyes were slitted as though he stared into something bright. "This time, I'll use some common sense. I guess I'm getting old. I no longer want to be big. I just want to make a good living. We can do that, if—" He choked and coughed.

Harl waited until the spasm passed. "What's that 'if'?"

"It all depends on how Ira sees it," Hiram replied. He searched for words, and Harl waited in stony silence. He felt no pity for his father, only a heavy censure.

"If Pike was still alive, I wouldn't have a worry in the world. I'd march in there and say, 'Pike, I need help. Can't pay you anything on that loan this year.'" He hawked and spit, then growled, "Pike would say, 'How long do you want, Hiram?' Just a few words would straighten out the whole matter. But now—" His words faltered and died.

"You're finally realizing we're dealing with Ira now," Harl said bitingly.

Hiram groaned hollowly. "By God, I'll make Ira listen. He

always struck me as not having much backbone. But since he inherited the bank, he might think he has to strut to impress people. I'll shake that idea out of his head in a hurry."

Once Hiram got a thought in his head, it lodged like a burr in a mustang's tail. Harl wanted to knock the present thought to shreds. "How do you intend to do that?" he asked caustically.

Hiram's hand brushed the butt of his gun. "I've used this before. I can use it again. I'll see how he acts when he looks down the barrel of this," he muttered.

"That would be smart," Harl exploded. "Quincy would be on your back before you could turn your head. He'd have to protect Ira. Do you want to make things worse by going to jail?"

Hiram's mouth worked violently. "Damned if I thought you'd take sides with somebody like Ira. You know I'm not wrong in this. It's all—"

"Save it," Harl said wearily. He knew what Hiram was going to say: everything he was doing was for Harl's sake. "You're just about as far wrong as you can be," Harl said. "I'm trying to think of Melody. She'd naturally be on her brother's side. Are you trying to turn her against me?"

Hiram ducked his head, and that could be shame on his face. "Oh hell, yes," he said and hit his forehead with the heel of his palm. "I wasn't thinking about her at all." He swallowed hard, and his eyes appealed to Harl for understanding. "I guess the winter has knocked your plans into a cocked hat."

"I told her that our plans would have to wait," Harl said dully. "I didn't know how bad the mess was until you told me. My God," he said frantically, "that puts our wedding off even further. I want a promise from you. I don't want you making things any worse." Harl's jaw was set hard. "I don't want you to shoot off your mouth in Ira's office. I'll be there to shut you up, if you start."

For a moment, raw temper flashed in Hiram's eyes. "By God, I ain't letting nobody take my ranch over something I can't help."

"Did you ever hear of the word compromise?" Harl asked coldly. "We're not there to ask for any more money. All we're asking for is a little more time."

Hiram nodded jerkily as though he had reached an abrupt decision. "I'll keep that in mind, son. All I want to do is to talk sense to Ira. If he ever heard the word," he finished gloomily.

This was the best Harl could do, but it still left him fearful. How would Hiram take it, if Ira got too mouthy? All he could do was to wait and see. He felt as though he were walking an icy path over a deep chasm, and every step carried him a little nearer to the brink.

"Maybe Ira won't be in," he said hopefully.

"You can bet he will," Hiram said despondently. "He knows what day it is as well as I do." He touched his horse's flanks with his spurs. "Let's get in and get this over."

Harl let Hiram spur ahead before he followed him. There went one tough, cantankerous old cuss. Hiram had always dug holes to fall into. Harl just prayed this hole wasn't too deep for Hiram to clamber out of. He lifted the reins and followed his father. He couldn't think of a time when he so dreaded a trip into Miles City.

Chapter Eight

When Temple entered his office, Newman was just depositing a huge armful of wood beside the stove.

"Morning, Mr. Temple," Newman greeted him.

Temple grunted in reply. About the only favorable thing he could say about Newman was that he kept the stove well supplied with wood.

Newman started to leave, and Temple stopped him. "Mungo, I want to talk to you."

Immediate concern registered on Newman's face. "Something wrong, Mr. Temple?"

People of Newman's class always lived as though some dread circumstance were on the verge of happening. "If there had been, I'd have told you," Temple said in irritation. "I want you to be especially watchful today. I expect Hiram Stark to come in."

There was a gleam in Newman's dull eyes. "Why today, sir?"

Temple shook his head impatiently. He knew all right, but he had no intention of telling Newman. A disturbing reaction ran through Temple. Stark might be able to make the payment. No, Temple thought in violent disagreement. Stark was in no better shape than anybody else.

"Just keep your eyes open, Mungo. I don't want Hiram walking into my office without you being around."

"Do you think he'll get in an argument with you, sir?"

"There's no telling what that crazy temper might force him to do," Temple snapped. "You just do what I hired you to do."

"You can depend on me," Newman said.

"All right," Temple said testily. He might need Newman for protection. Hiram could lose all reason when Temple announced he was foreclosing on him. Temple's lips felt stiff, and he forced them to move. "Watch every move Stark makes. At the first sign of him turning violent, I want you to do whatever is necessary to stop him. Have you got that straight?"

Newman nodded vigorously. "I've got it, sir. You don't have to worry."

"Good," Temple exclaimed. He briskly rubbed his hands together. They seemed suddenly chilly. It was odd; the room had felt unbearably warm when he came in.

He walked with Newman to the door. "Remember, I'm depending on you."

Newman bobbed his head. "You can rely on me, Mr. Temple."

Temple slapped Newman on the shoulder. "I knew I could."

He closed the door behind Newman and leaned against it. He didn't know why, but his knees felt suddenly weak. What would Hiram do when Temple announced he faced a foreclosure? Temple wiped a shaky hand across his brow.

Newman walked over to the teller's cage. He knew Duncan didn't care for him, but he asked, "Charley, will you help me keep an eye out for Hiram Stark? If he does come in, I wouldn't want to miss him."

Duncan cocked an eye at him. "Why?" he asked bluntly.

Newman slowly shook his head. "I'm not sure, but Mr. Temple is afraid of trouble. He told me that Mr. Stark could lose his head and blow off."

Duncan snorted in derision. "Pure imagination. I've known Hiram Stark for a long time. Sure, he's got a tough temper, but usually with a reason. What did Ira say the reason would be?"

"Mr. Temple didn't say. He just warned me to watch out for him."

"Then it's up to you to keep your eyes open," Duncan snapped. "Don't go to sleep standing against the wall."

"I don't do that," Newman said, offended. "I think I'm doing a good job."

"Then you'd better start doing it," Duncan growled. He turned his attention back to his work, dismissing Newman from his mind.

Duncan didn't know anybody was near until a voice said, "How are things going, Charley?"

Duncan looked up into Hiram Stark's face. Harl was beside him.

"Pretty good," Duncan said slowly. His eyes went to Newman. There was no need to tell him the Starks were here. Newman intently watched them, and his eyes glittered.

"Got to see Ira," Hiram said.

Duncan bobbed his head. "Go right on in," he said.

He watched them walk to Ira's door. He turned his head, and Newman was closing the distance between them. Duncan wanted to yell his protest, but he bit back the words. It was none of his affair.

His eyes were glued to Newman and the two men he followed. It looked as though Newman intended following the Starks into Ira's office. Duncan shrugged. If Ira didn't want Newman in there, he could order him out.

Newman had almost caught up with the two as Hiram reached for the doorknob. Neither of the Starks paid him any attention. Newman stepped through the door right on the Starks' heels.

Chapter Nine

Hiram and Harl didn't realize Newman was right behind them until they were inside Temple's office. The scrape of Newman's boots reached Hiram, and he whipped his head around. Surprise swept across his face. He looked back at Temple and blurted, "What the hell?"

Temple waved an expansive hand, though he seemed tight. "Just a new precaution I've added, Hiram. Mungo comes into my office on every important transaction. It protects the bank's and the customers' interests."

Hiram's face darkened. "Sounds like a lot of foolishness to me. Damn it! I want some privacy on my personal affairs."

"I'm surprised to hear that," Temple said glibly. "You're the first to complain."

Harl glanced at his father. Hiram's face was darkening. Hiram had forgotten his promise. Harl tried to get his attention and shook his head. If Hiram saw the warning, nothing registered on his face. Just a little thing such as the precaution of this new guard irritated him.

"Ira, I don't like another person sitting in listening to my personal business," Hiram growled.

"Harl's with you," Temple pointed out.

Hiram snorted. "Harl's part of the family. He's got a right."

"Well, Mungo is part of the bank family," Temple countered. Hiram's absurd stand was arousing his own temper. Hiram had no right to try and dictate the way he ran his bank. Temple leaned forward, his face flaming. "Did you come in to just complain about the way I run my business?" he demanded.

"I came in to talk about something pretty serious to me," Hiram said heatedly.

Harl kept clearing his throat and throwing Hiram pleading glances, but Hiram ignored them. Each glance screamed, "Ease down, Pa. You came in to ask a favor of Ira. You're not going to get it if you make him mad."

Hiram's abrupt nod told Harl he'd caught the message. He sat down before the desk and placed both hands on its polished surface. He drew a deep breath and said, "Ira, I came in to ask a tremendous favor."

"Everybody's asking me favors," Temple said petulantly. He was still upset, and he took little pain to hide the feeling.

Hiram clamped his lips together, bunching the muscles in his jaw. A wave of blood turned his face almost black, and he looked ready to explode.

"Pa," Harl said more sharply this time.

Hiram fought a mighty battle to control himself and leaned back in his chair. He was too angry to notice Newman's movement. Newman had moved a pace forward, and there seemed to be a sense of anticipation in him.

Hiram tried hard to get the conversation back on a friendly basis. "Ira, you know how bad last winter was."

"I should," Temple said crisply. "I went through it, too. Everybody who comes in here tells me about it."

Hiram was having trouble with his breathing, and his face looked congested.

Temple's deliberately trying to rile Pa, Harl thought.

"Don't get smart with me, Ira," Hiram snapped. "I wasn't trying to be funny. I was just making a statement."

Temple glanced at Newman, then his attention went back to Hiram. "I heard what you said. Surely, you didn't come in here just to talk about the weather."

Hiram's eyes turned smoky, but he was doing a remarkable job of controlling his temper. "I have a reason," he said curtly. His sigh sounded as though it came from the pit of his stomach. "It sure was different talking to your father," he said morosely.

Harl's eyes shifted from Hiram to Temple. The more he observed, the more he felt Temple was deliberately trying to rile Hiram. It didn't make sense, but Harl could reach no other conclusion. These two stubborn people could tongue-lash each other into a stand from which neither could retreat. Harl had to prevent that. "Pa, tell Ira what you want and get it over with."

Hiram coughed several times and hacked to clear his throat.

"I lost a lot of cattle last winter, Ira."

"Who didn't?" Temple asked indifferently.

That fierce flame reappeared in Hiram's eyes. Harl couldn't believe his ears. Temple was making this as difficult as he could. Harl sucked in a troubled breath, waiting for Hiram to react to Temple's manner.

"I ain't no different than anybody else," Hiram growled. "What's got into you? I never had no trouble talking to your father."

"Pike and I saw things differently," Temple said impatiently. "You've done a hell of lot of talking but so far you haven't said anything."

Hiram half-heaved himself out of his chair, then relaxed and slowly sank back. He breathed hard, and his voice was strained. "You make it tough to talk to you, Ira. If you want it straight, here it is. I was supposed to pay a thousand dollars on my mortgage today."

Temple nodded. His eyes were mere slits, and he watched Hiram warily. "Yes," he agreed, "on a total loan of twelve thousand dollars."

"I know how that mortgage reads," Hiram said testily.

"Good," Temple boomed. "Then there can be no disagreement between us."

Hiram leaned forward, and his figure was rigid. "If I miss

a payment, then the whole amount comes due," he said in a dead voice. "I haven't got that payment."

"That's too bad," Temple purred. "You know what happens now."

Hiram's face looked as though it were carved out of stone. "Suppose you tell me."

"Then I'll have to foreclose on you, Hiram. You knew all those conditions when Pike made you that loan. It's a standard clause, used in all banks to protect a bank's money."

Harl was proud of his father. Hiram took that blow without visible flinching.

Hiram raised his hands in a helpless gesture. "All I'm asking is for an extension. I may be able to pay you a few dollars on the interest, but the rest is going to have to slide for a year."

He stared disbelievingly at Temple. Temple was slowly shaking his head, and there was an ugly determination in the gesture.

"What do you mean, no?" Hiram's voice rose until he was almost screaming. "I've done a lot of business through the years with this bank. I think I've earned better handling than this. I'm not asking you to give me any money. I'm merely asking you to postpone this year's payment." Temple kept staring at him, and Hiram said, "Why damn it. Pike wouldn't have told me no."

"Pike's not here," Temple said brusquely. "I'm running this bank now. Pike did a lot of things we disagreed over." Temple shook his head with more vehemence. "I can't do it," he snapped. "A bank isn't a charitable institution."

Hiram jumped to his feet, his face contorted. "Nobody's going to take my ranch," he said furiously.

Temple's eyes fired with an evil light. "Just wait and see, Hiram."

Hiram leaned far over the desk, and Temple shoved his chair back as far as he could. By the strained expression on his face, he expected all hell to break loose.

A severe spell of coughing broke up Hiram's attempt to say something more. His face congested with color, and he choked. His hand brushed away the skirts of his sheepskin, and his fingers fumbled at his hip pocket.

Newman lunged forward, his face wild. "Here now!" he roared. "Hold it!"

Hiram threw him a surprised look, but Newman's protest didn't stop him fumbling for a handkerchief.

Harl read Newman's expression correctly, and he felt his heart freeze. That damned fool was reaching for his gun.

"Don't." Harl screamed at the top of his lung. "Pa's only reaching for a handkerchief—" He never got to finish the sentence.

Newman jerked out his gun and threw down on Hiram. The report of the gun sounded inordinately loud in the confines of the room. Powder smoke filled the air. Harl watched with sick eyes as Hiram staggered under the impact of a bullet in his back. Hiram's eyes were shocked and pleading. He rocked back and forth on the balls of his feet. A thin trickle of blood ran down from a lip corner. He came apart all at once and fell limply like a half-filled grain sack.

Chapter Ten

For a long, agonizing moment, Harl couldn't move. His eyes were riveted to the motionless figure on the floor. He knew with a terrible certainty Hiram was dead. The moment wiped out all the discord between them. Grief and rage poured through him. This was his father.

Harl looked at Newman, and his face was stamped with such fury that Newman instinctively shrank back from him.

"Goddamn you," Harl said in a broken voice. "You killed him."

Newman was terrified. He tried to speak, and spittle sprayed the air. He kept moving his lips, but no sound came out. Finally, he managed to say, "I had to," he said in a faltering voice. "You saw it all. You saw him reach for his gun."

Harl was shaking like a leaf in a high wind. In another shattering moment, he would turn into a maniac with a wild desire to destroy Newman.

"He was reaching for a handkerchief!" Harl screamed. "You heard him cough."

Newman rubbed the back of his left hand across his eyes. He gasped for breath and stammered, "He was reaching for a gun. Ask Mr. Temple. He saw it all."

The red haze grew thicker before Harl's eyes, and he lost all control. "Hiram didn't come in here looking for a gun fight. You miserable son of a bitch. I'm going to tear your head off."

The fact that Newman held a gun didn't deter Harl. He ran the few steps between him and Newman, his head bel-

ligerently thrust forward. His shoulders were bunched, and
his hands opened and closed. An insane rage stamped his
face.

Newman side-stepped that first rush, and Harl's eagerness
to get at him made him rush past Newman. He checked his
momentum and tried to whirl. Newman brought the gun
barrel down in a vicious, chopping stroke, and it thudded
against Harl's hat, crushing it flat against his head. The blow
took all the co-ordination out of Harl's muscles. He fought
to retain his balance, but his legs had turned into rubbery,
treacherous things, refusing to support him. He fell face forward, crashing against the floor.

Temple jumped to his feet, and his breathing made a
jerky, rasping sound. "You've done it now!" he yelled at
Newman.

Newman's eyes flicked from one prone figure to the other.
His face drained of all color.

"You saw it all," he gasped. "He tried to pull a gun. I beat
him. That's all. I did it in your defense."

Temple shook his head but didn't comment. Maybe Newman thought Hiram was grabbing for a gun, but his gun was
still in its holster. This could be a god-awful mess.

"For your sake, I hope you're right," he said crisply.

He turned his head toward the babbling voice outside of
the door. That would be Duncan drawn by the report of the
gun.

Temple walked to the door, jerked it open, and said, "Get
that scared look off your face, Charley. I'm all right. Go and
get Quincy. We've got something bad in here. Damn it!
Don't stand there. Move!"

The sharp command broke Charley's trance. He backed
away, his eyes darting from Hiram to Harl.

Temple's voice crackled with authority. "I said move." He
waited until Charley ran toward the entrance, then closed
the door. He didn't want any curiosity seekers crowding into
his office.

He looked at Newman, his eyes judging. "You better put that damned thing away," he said dryly, "unless you intend to use it again."

Newman dropped the gun into its holster and looked at Temple with dumb, stricken eyes. "I thought he was drawing," he mumbled. A small flame of anger flared in his eyes. "You told me he was a hot-tempered man. You made me believe you expected violence from him. When he reached for his hip pocket, I thought he was grabbing for his gun. I was only trying to protect you."

Temple shook his head. "Talking like this will only dig your hole deeper. I'd advise you to say as little as possible."

Newman was scared. "My God, Mr. Temple, what am I going to do?"

"The first thing you're going to do is get hold of yourself. I don't want you punished for doing your duty. Let me think a minute."

He sat down and stared at the ceiling. He could hear Newman's agitated breathing and the shuffling of his feet as he moved nervously.

Temple looked at Newman and murmured, "Harl claims that Hiram was reaching for a handkerchief. Maybe we'd better go on the assumption Hiram wasn't reaching for a gun."

Newman turned a chalky white. "Oh, my God," he whispered. "If he wasn't reaching for a gun, then I'm a goner. The law will come down on me hard. I'd better get out of here."

"Running will do you far more harm than staying. They'd be after you, and they wouldn't stop until they run you down. Running will be a flat admission that you're guilty."

"What can I do?" Newman begged.

"I've been thinking about that," Temple replied. "First, check and see if Harl was lying about the handkerchiefs."

Newman bent over Hiram and ran his hands over Hiram's

body. He searched every pocket, and he looked sick as he looked up at Temple.

"His hip pocket was filled with handkerchiefs," he said, his lips trembling. "It looks like Harl was right."

"Could be," Temple said in agreement. "Maybe we can do something about that." He bent over and jerked Hiram's gun out of its holster. He laid it on the floor inches from Hiram's right hand.

Temple straightened, cocking his head, studying his work. "That makes it look more credible," he murmured. "You didn't draw until Hiram pulled his own gun. It takes the blame off of you. You thought Hiram was drawing on you, and you protected your own life. Just remember that. You say nothing more when Rader gets here. Do you understand what I'm telling you?"

Newman stubbornly shook his head. "I ain't going to jail for this. I'm not taking the sole blame."

The wrong words could send Newman into headlong flight. Temple's voice dropped to a conciliatory tone. "I don't want you going to jail. I'll get the best lawyer I can hire. If it comes to the worst, I think the sentence will be easy. I'd guess six months or no more than a year."

"No," Newman said stubbornly. "I ain't going to pay it alone."

Temple made a steeple of his fingers and peered over it at Newman. "If you are sentenced, I'll make it worth your while. Outside of admitting you shot Hiram Stark because you thought he was drawing a gun, say nothing."

"No," Newman said with the same degree of stubbornness. "I'm not going to take all the blame."

Temple's lips were a tightly clamped line. This man had the stubbornness of a mule. "Do you think I want to see things turn out bad for you? After all, you were trying to protect me. I want to turn this to your advantage."

Newman struggled to regain control of his jerky breathing. "How could that be?"

"If you do exactly as I say, I'm willing to pay you twenty-five hundred dollars for serving whatever sentence a judge might hand you."

Newman's eyes went round in awe. Twenty-five hundred was a tremendous sum of money. He licked his lips and asked, "If it goes against me at the trial, how long did you say I'd have to serve?"

Temple pulled at an ear lobe. "Not more than a year. I think the judge will decide this case is an accident. Twenty-five hundred is pretty good pay for a year."

Newman struggled against making such a rough decision. "You think the most I'd have to serve would be a year?"

Temple shrugged. "Hell, Mungo, you know I can't guarantee you anything. The way it happened, I'd say a year is a likely sentence."

Newman's forehead was deeply furrowed as he considered what Temple said. The sum Temple mentioned would be more than enough to take care of Ruby. Knowing that she would get along wiped some of the pressure from his mind.

He squinted at Temple. "Would you give the money to Ruby? Without me, she wouldn't have anything to live on."

"I'd be glad to," Temple said heartily. "The minute the judge sets your sentence I'll see that she gets the money."

Newman didn't like the way everything was closing in on him, but there was one bright spot. If it wasn't for Temple's generosity, he would be in a desperate hole.

He started to say something when Harl groaned.

"Hold it," Temple said. "Harl's come to. Do we have an agreement?"

"I guess we do," Newman said feebly.

Harl was reviving. He ran a hand over his eyes, and his breathing quickened. He looked vaguely about him as though he couldn't quite focus on anything definite. His eyes traveled around the room and fixed on Newman. Everything came back to him in a rush, and he tried to sit up.

"Damn you, Newman," he said passionately. "I'll pay you back for this."

He didn't have enough strength to rise. He turned over and got his arms under him. He raised his torso from the floor, but his arms weren't strong enough to push his weight all the way up. They buckled, and he went flat again.

"Just give me a minute," he said wrathfully. "I'll make it. I'll take care of you."

"There's no sense in that kind of talk," Temple said sharply.

Harl glared at him. "Do you expect me to forget that bastard killed my father?"

"I've already done something about that," Temple said consolingly. "Charley has gone after the sheriff. We'll let Rader handle this from now on."

Harl turned over and sat up. His eyes were hot coals, raking Temple. "What part did you have in this, Ira? When I find out, I promise you, you'll be damned sorry."

"Don't threaten me," Temple said heatedly. "Your pa started all this trouble. He was in a quarrelsome mood when he came in. You were here; you heard him. Mungo was afraid for me. When he saw Hiram go for his gun, he acted naturally."

Harl's strength had returned, and he was able to scramble to his feet. "That's a goddamned lie, Ira. I've told you before, Hiram was only reaching for a handkerchief." He glanced at Hiram, and his eyes misted. Harl angrily shook his head. He noticed something he hadn't seen before. Hiram's gun lay on the floor near his hand. Harl was positive Hiram hadn't touched the weapon. His eyes sharpened as he looked at Temple and Newman. They were the only other two people in the room. One of them had removed the gun from the holster and placed it on the floor. Temple or Newman? Harl didn't know. He almost blurted out the accusation, but he clamped his lips tight. From now on, he was going to do his talking only with Quincy Rader present.

There was a loud knocking at the door; he whipped his head around. An angry voice on the other side of the door carried clearly to Harl. "Oh hell, Charley. You may have to knock to get permission to enter this office—I haven't got the time to play such games. Or the inclination," he added.

The door was flung open, and Duncan was shoved out of the way. Quincy Rader stomped into the room. He stopped short of Hiram's body, and his eyes were narrowed and speculative.

For a moment, the silence was heavy. Rader was shorter than the average, but his width more than made up for the height discrepancy. Rader was a good man with a nerve that never weakened no matter what he went up against.

Rader raised his head, and his eyes were angry as he looked at Temple. "So it finally happened, Ira. I told you I was against a special guard going around with hardware on his hip. I told you, you didn't need a guard. It finally got a man killed."

Temple flushed at the acrimony in Rader's voice. "Don't go jumping to any conclusions, Quincy. I thought the bank and I needed protection." He nodded smugly. "From what just happened, I'd say I was right."

Rader threw up a hand, checking anything else Temple might intend to say. "Harl, did you see this?"

"I did." Harl's voice was cracked by anger and grief. "Pa was just talking to Temple when all of a sudden that bastard over there pulled out his gun and shot Pa." Harl's face twisted under a rush of grief. "I saw Pa fall and made a rush for Newman. He hit me with his gun barrel and knocked me cold."

Rader turned accusing eyes on Newman. "What caused you to draw on him?"

Newman held out pleading hands. "What else could I believe but that there was danger in the man. He got in a heated argument with Mr. Temple. The longer it went on, the more heated it became."

Temple broke in, drawing Rader's scowl. "Hiram was losing his head. He looked crazy, and he could scarcely control his voice. I don't blame Mungo for feeling like he did. When Hiram made a gesture toward his hip pocket, I guess Mungo thought it was time to stop him."

Harl was furious. He had never heard more lies in a single statement.

Rader held up a hand, stopping Harl's outburst. "Hold it, Harl. You'll get your turn." He looked back at Temple. "What was the argument about, Ira?"

Temple looked as though the seat of his chair were suddenly uncomfortable. "Hiram wanted a year's extension on his loan. He lost his head when I refused to listen. Hell, a bank can't be run that way."

"You're a goddamned liar," Harl said with cold ferocity. "If you're going to talk, get it straight." He watched Temple squirm for a moment, then said contemptuously, "Looks like he doesn't want to tell the truth, or it isn't in him."

"Easy, Harl," Rader cautioned. He didn't want this to break down into a jawbone fight with everybody hurling accusations at each other without proof or basis.

"Pa did ask for an extension," Harl said, breathing more quietly. "The winter hurt us. We lost a lot of cattle. Hiram didn't figure he was asking for too much. He did business with Pike for a long time. All he was asking for was a favor." Those accusatory eyes fixed on Temple. "Pike would have jumped at the chance to do that favor. This one"—he put all his contempt into the two words—"wouldn't even listen."

"Did he yell at Ira?" Rader questioned.

"Yes," Harl admitted. "And I don't blame him. Ira didn't even try to work out things with him. He just said a flat no." His eyes were baleful as he glanced at Temple.

"Newman said something about Hiram grabbing at his hip pocket," Rader said. "Was that true?"

"True enough," Harl said steadily. "Pa's been fighting a bad cold the whole winter. He carried fresh handkerchiefs in his hip pocket." His voice was getting thick, threatening to break. "I guess he wanted to clear his head before he could go on."

"Aw, come on, Harl," Rader protested. "Hiram's gun is lying right beside him. He must have drawn it."

Harl's face was stony cold. "I'll tell you about that later, Quincy."

"Somebody here's lying," Rader said thoughtfully. "A smarter head than mine will have to find out who. It'll all come out in the trial."

"You're going to try Mungo?" Temple cried.

"Not me," Rader corrected. "The judge will do that." He was suddenly angered. "A man's been killed here. Do you expect me to just forget it?"

Temple shrank back in his chair. "I guess not," he said weakly.

"Give me your gun," Rader said coldly. He took the weapon from Newman's hand, looked at it, then dropped the gun into his coat pocket. "You're going with me, Newman. You're under arrest."

"You can't arrest him for doing his duty," Temple cried.

"Watch me," Rader said sardonically. "You coming, Harl?"

Harl shook his head. "I'm staying with Hiram."

"All right," Rader agreed. "But watch your step, Harl. I don't want any quarreling with Ira. I expect you to come down to the office."

The words wanted to clog in Harl's throat. "I'll be down just as soon as Hiram is taken care of."

"Good," Rader replied. He shoved Newman toward the door. "Get moving, Newman."

Chapter Eleven

Harl watched the door close on Rader and Newman. He glanced at Temple who seemed to be fidgeting unnecessarily.

"Why are you staring at me?" Temple asked hotly.

"Does it bother you that much?" Harl asked in a low voice. "I wonder if Rader took the wrong man."

"What the hell does that mean?"

"Take it any way you want," Harl said ominously.

A fiery red fought with the chalky white of Temple's face. "Are you accusing me of something?"

"You think I should?" Harl asked softly.

Temple's face purpled. "Get out of my office!" he yelled.

"Yell your damned head off," Harl said firmly. "I'm not leaving until I can take Pa with me."

Temple failed to meet Harl's eyes. He tried to salvage something out of his defeat. "What happened doesn't change anything," he said savagely. "Your payment is still due."

"You've said that before," Harl said wearily.

Duncan still stood in the doorway, taking in all of this.

"Charley," Harl said. "Do me a favor, will you? Go down and get Wilkie for me. Tell him I want him to pick up Hiram."

Duncan left, closing the door behind him.

Harl tried to avoid looking at Hiram. He could hear Temple squirming in his chair. He had never been able to say he liked Temple; now his dislike mounted to a full-fledged hatred. Was this just a simple case of Newman losing his head and shooting, or was it something darker and deeper? Harl's suspicions kept mounting. He knew that Hiram hadn't drawn his gun. Still, Rader had found a gun beside Hiram's body. Either Temple or Newman was responsible for pulling Hiram's gun from its holster and placing it beside him. Temple knew what had happened.

Harl's mind beat at the murky surface. Was Hiram's killing part of a well-thought-out scheme? At first, he rejected the thought. Temple didn't have the backbone to take a major part in Hiram's deliberate killing. Harl's mind pried at the few, scanty facts he had. If Temple wanted the Bow Gun badly enough, Harl's suspicion that Temple was in some way involved might have some basis in fact.

He sat there, staring at Temple, and the scrutiny unnerved Temple.

"Why are you staring at me?" Temple repeated. His voice kept rising until it sounded like a squeal.

"Maybe you know the answer to that better than I do, Ira." Harl leveled a finger at Temple. "This isn't settled yet, Ira. Your part in this will eventually come out."

Temple's voice picked up a bluster. "You're making accusations without proof. I can sue you for that."

Harl smiled bleakly. "We'll see, Ira. I think a lot of things are going to come out in that court."

Harl didn't speak again, but his eyes never left Temple. Temple's agitation became more apparent, and small beads of sweat broke out on his forehead.

You're involved in some way, Harl thought. I'll find out. The promise was vague and unsatisfying.

Harl turned his head at the sound of footsteps. Duncan was coming through the door, and the undertaker was with him.

Wilkie was a rotund man with a completely bald head. He had two expressions, one of sorrow for moments like this, and his everyday expression. The pretended sorrow made his face look long and lugubrious.

"I can't tell you how sorry I am about this, Harl—"

The slash of Harl's hand cut off the rest of what Wilkie wanted to say. Wilkie could be long winded, if he had the chance.

"Appreciate it, Sam," Harl said gruffly, "but it's done and can't be recalled."

Wilkie threw him an injured glance. He had a set speech for moments like this, and Harl wasn't going to stop him from saying it. "Terrible shock, Harl. Your only consolation is that you had him all these years. And he's gone to a better place. When Charley told me what happened, I brought the hearse with me," he added.

"Good." Harl approved. "I'll give you a hand."

He and Wilkie carried Hiram out to the old hearse with its huge glass windows. Harl learned how difficult it was to handle an inert body. He had a dull ache inside him, but he felt no real grief. Hiram had used too harsh a hand on him during the growing up years. He wondered how much grief Addie would feel. Hiram had been an opinionated man, and often his handling of his wife was rough. Harl supposed that like him Addie would know her share of sorrow, but there could also be a sense of relief.

Harl rode beside Wilkie to his establishment. He stared straight ahead, though he was well aware that everybody they passed turned and gawked after them.

Harl helped Wilkie get Hiram inside and carry him into that bleak rear room.

"Put Hiram in the best coffin you have, Sam," Harl ordered. "Bring him out to the ranch. Hiram would prefer to be buried out there."

After he left Wilkie, Harl walked down the street to Rader's office. Quincy was behind his desk, deep in thought.

"Have any trouble with Newman, Quincy?"

"Him?" Rader said scornfully. "Newman was never anything but a husk wrapped around a lot of brag."

"He still claiming that Hiram drew first?"

"He told it so many times, I got sick of listening to it." He stopped, his eyes boring into Harl, as he waited.

Harl thought briefly about the best way to present his story, then he said slowly, "I know Hiram wore a gun into town. But that was strictly from habit. He had no intention of using it." He bristled at Rader's look of doubt. "Damn it, Quincy! I was there. I know what happened. Doesn't it strike you odd that Hiram was shot in the back?"

Rader's doubting look didn't ease too much. "Hiram did attempt to draw," Rader said reasonably. "His gun was beside him."

Harl shrugged in irritation. "Pa was reaching into his hip pocket for a handkerchief. He was arguing with Ira so much he got all choked up."

"I found the handkerchiefs," Rader said. "He had four or five. He must have been fighting a bad cold."

Rader's tone had changed, and Harl relaxed. "He was, Quincy. I'm not trying to deny that Newman mistook Pa's grab for a handkerchief as a reach for his gun."

"That doesn't explain the gun lying beside Hiram," Rader pointed out.

Harl shook his head. "He didn't touch that gun," he said wearily.

Skepticism remained in Rader's eyes. "You got a reasonable explanation for the gun, Harl?"

Harl's cheeks hollowed with the suck of air into his lungs. Here was the part that could be difficult for Rader to believe. "I think Temple or Newman pulled Hiram's gun out of his holster and laid it beside him," he said slowly.

Rader whistled softly and shook his head.

Harl felt his cheeks heat up. "Is Temple too important a man to accuse of wrong doing?" he asked bluntly.

Rader's face turned bleak, and his eyes were cold and savage. "You know better than that, Harl."

"I guess I'm kinda worked up, Quincy."

"Every right to be," Rader acknowledged. "Did you ac-

cuse Ira of removing Hiram's gun? You didn't say anything
while I was in his office."

"I didn't," Harl admitted. "Ira would only deny it. I
wanted to talk it over with you."

"I'm glad you didn't say anything," Rader said. "I hate
the idea of giving Ira an advance warning, if he is involved.
Your accusation could put him on guard."

Harl felt his hopes revive. "You think he might be behind
all this?"

"Not ready to go that far yet," Rader replied. "Did Hiram
own the Bow Gun outright?"

"Not quite," Harl answered. "He borrowed twelve thousand dollars on the place before Pike died. His first payment
was due today. That's why he was in the bank, to ask Ira for
an extension of time."

"Ah," Rader said thoughtfully. "Was that the basis of the
argument?"

"Mostly. Hiram went wild when Ira mentioned foreclosure. I suspect that was the cause of his coughing. He
reached for a handkerchief, and Newman shot him."

Rader was silent for so long that Harl began to feel that
Rader believed him. "Pike would have granted that extension, Quincy."

"I don't doubt it," Rader replied dryly. His fingers
drummed on his desk. "Two different people. Harl, do you
realize what you're saying?"

The softness of the question startled Harl. "All this might
have been planned?"

"I'm beginning to get a bad feeling about Ira. Like a
snake crawling across my chest."

A strengthening hope was a hard throb inside Harl.
"Hiram claimed his cold was an echo of the winter."

Rader nodded. "He could be right. A bad disturbance like
that winter can arouse a lot of echoes in many ways."

Harl leaned forward, his body going tense. "What are you
trying to say, Quincy?"

"I don't know yet, Harl. But hiring Newman could be the beginning of it all." Rader said crossly at the blankness remaining on Harl's face, "Don't you see it yet? Ira could be beset with ambition. I started worrying about how the bank would be run, right after Pike died. Ira was never the man his father was. Ira never liked the way Pike held him down. He always wanted to be something bigger than he was."

"Why, goddamn him," Harl said explosively.

"Guessing isn't proof," Rader pointed out.

"He hired Newman, didn't he?"

"You're rushing things again," Rader said in rebuke. "I talked to Ira about hiring Newman. He insisted he needed all the protection he could get. When he hired Newman, did he have a thought of getting rid of Hiram? It's an interesting question."

Harl slammed the desk with the heel of his hand. "I'm not going to let it stop here, Quincy."

Rader nodded. "Didn't expect you to. But you're not going to rush into making accusations that would put Ira on his guard. We'll see what comes out at Newman's trial."

Harl managed a shaky grin. Rader was behind him. He stood and said, "I'll leave it in your hands, Quincy. I've got to get back to Wilkie's. He's taking care of Hiram. I'm going to have Wilkie drive Hiram out to the ranch."

"He would like that, Harl. He sure wouldn't rest easy on some alien land." He walked to the door with Harl. "Just take it easy, Harl. Anderson will prosecute the case against Newman. Andy's got a sharp mind behind those sleepy eyes."

"Are you going to tell him what we talked about?"

"I'm going to lay out everything I know or guess at about Ira," Rader said firmly.

Chapter Twelve

Addie saw the hearse drive into the yard. She flew out of the house before Harl climbed down.

Harl put an arm about her shoulders. "Easy, Ma."

Her lips trembled, and her eyes were distraught, but outside of those telltale signs, Harl could see no threatening breakdown. "Is it Hiram?" Her voice was a dry, thin whisper, like the sound of two old leaves rubbing each other.

"Yes, Ma."

Now the breakdown would come, and Harl waited for it. Addie seemed to reach deep inside herself and draw on a new source of strength. She looked full into Harl's face, and her eyes were dry.

"His temper cause it, Harl?" she asked quietly.

Harl hesitated, seeking the kindest way to tell her.

His delay angered Addie, and she said, "I've got the right to know."

"You have, Ma." At the moment, she looked so thin and frail, and he marveled at her fortitude.

"He didn't seek a quarrel, Ma. All he wanted was an extension of his mortgage with Ira. Ira's hired security guard mistook Hiram's gesture as a threat."

"You saw it?"

Harl nodded slowly. "Hiram was reaching for a handkerchief. That's all."

"Was he quarreling with Ira?" Her question was sharp and to the point.

"I guess you could call it that," Harl admitted. "When Ira said something about foreclosing, Hiram's face was flushed.

He choked and reached for a handkerchief. That guard read the signs all wrong."

"What's your opinion, Harl?"

He considered his reply carefully, wondering how far he should go. He decided upon complete honesty. There had never been any subterfuge between them.

"It was almost like Ira was waiting for what happened. I jumped for the guard, and he clubbed me down with his gun barrel."

"Are you hurt?" she asked in quick concern.

He shook his head. "My hat softened the blow. When I came to, Quincy was there. Ira had sent for him."

"Was Ira fearful?" Addie asked.

"Why should he be?" Harl answered bitterly. "He wasn't the one who killed Hiram. No blame could touch him."

"That your feeling, Harl?"

"Yes," he said flatly. "Ira still demands the payment, or he'll foreclose. It looks like Ira sees a good chance to take over the Bow Gun."

"I'd hate that, Harl." Addie's voice picked up a grim note. "I came to Montana with Hiram and helped him establish the Bow Gun. He wouldn't want some hard-nosed banker getting it that easily."

"Quincy sees it that way, too."

"That makes me feel better," she said quickly. "What do you plan to do?"

"Right now, bury Hiram. Wilkie's beginning to fidget. He wants to get back to town."

Her nod came without hesitation. "Do you want to call the hands?"

"I'd better," he replied. "There's a lot of work ahead."

Addie shivered, and Harl wondered if that was the first sign of weakening. But her words denied that. "The wind's chilling, Harl. I'm going back to the house and get a wrap. Call me when you're ready."

He squeezed her hand in understanding and watched

her return to the house. Her shoulders were squared, and her step was firm. There went one tough lady, Harl thought, then turned to the bunkhouse. The six riders were inside, and one look at Harl's tense face told them that something bad had happened. The winter had dwindled the original work force. Of a dozen riders, only six remained. Two had died during the winter, and the other four had drifted to a gentler climate.

Cully, the foreman, broke the silence after studying Harl's face. "What's happened, Harl?"

"Hiram's been shot."

He saw the varying emotions on the watching faces. Shock, yes, but little grief. These men had no love for Hiram. His temper was too unpredictable, but they did have respect for him.

"How did it happen, Harl?" Cully asked.

"Some gun-crazy guard in the bank cut down on him," Harl replied. He didn't want to go into details again. After a story was retold several times, a man grew thoroughly weary of it.

That wasn't enough to satisfy their curiosity, and Harl said, "Rader put the guard under arrest. He'll stand trial."

Heads around the semicircle bobbed. Now they could relax. "Where's Hiram?" Hebb asked.

"Wilkie brought him home, Hebb."

"Hiram would have liked that," Hebb said solemnly.

Harl watched the nods of agreement and thought, if a man couldn't win another's liking, then respect was the next best thing.

"I'll need some help getting the grave ready," Harl said.

He got six offers, and his throat went tight. It was a final tribute to Hiram.

The ground was moist, almost muddy, and the digging wasn't hard. Six willing pairs of hands completed the job quickly.

Harl looked at the raw wound in the earth and suddenly

realized the extent of his loss. His father was gone. All the memories of the good times flashed through his mind. Hiram had taught him how to ride, how to shoot, in fact, how to grow up. Of course, the teaching hadn't been gentle, and a small wonder ran through Harl's mind. What kind of a man would he have been if it hadn't been for Hiram's rough handling?

"I've got to go get Ma," he said through a tight throat.

He plodded toward the house, afraid that Addie had broken down. Once curious eyes were no longer on her, those hard barriers might have fallen.

Harl found her sitting in a chair in the parlor. Her face was calm enough, but he sensed a strain in her.

"This was Hiram's favorite chair," she said in a barely audible boice. She angrily tossed her head at the weakness. Harl saw the glistening tears in her eyes. There was a softness in her.

Addie thumbed the moisture from her eyes. "I think I knew all along it would end this way. Hiram could be a violent man when his temper was aroused."

"Easy, Ma," Harl begged.

She seemed to ignore him, lost in her own thoughts. "Isn't it odd that at times like this, you remember only the goodness, the softness."

Harl nodded somberly. He had just experienced the same feeling. Sentimentality was a great shredder of dignity. He was afraid that was happening to Addie now.

"They're waiting for us, Ma," he prodded gently.

"Yes." Her voice was completely changed. It was tough again with no weakness in it. "I'll get a heavier coat and my hat," she said.

She joined Harl at the front door. She was pale but completely under control. Harl was proud of her.

Addie tucked her hand under Harl's arm and walked with him to the gravesite. "I didn't take time to find a minister," Harl whispered.

"Hiram would be unhappy if you *had* found one," she said in a tight voice. "He wasn't much of a believer anyway."

Harl kept his face straight. So she knew about Hiram's lack of belief. A man didn't slip much by an observant woman.

"Wilkie will say something," Addie assured Harl.

Wilkie took her hand as they came up, and the sorrowful words poured out of him. "I can't tell you how sorry I am, Mrs. Stark."

"Then don't try," she said crisply.

Harl caught grins on the faces of the nearby riders and barely managed to restrain his own smile. In her way, she was as tough as Hiram had ever been.

The riders carried the coffin out of the hearse and put it near the grave. "I'll get some rope," Cully said.

Harl nodded.

Nobody spoke as the coffin was lowered into the grave.

"If you want me to say something?" Wilkie ventured.

"We would, Sam," Harl replied gravely.

"Dear God," Wilkie intoned, "he comes seeking a better place. This was one of the true pioneers of Montana. He wrestled this land from the Indians and helped bring law and justice to the country. If he was tough, it was only because he had to be."

Harl thought Wilkie's words would never end. He shifted his weight from one foot to the other. He glanced at Addie, fearing this long-windedness would tear her down. Her face remained stoically composed, but Harl could swear that the setting sun picked up a glint of moisture in her eyes.

Harl wanted to get this over with so he could take Addie back to the house. He was sure her grip on his arm tightened. He was equally positive that old memories kept flashing through her mind. He ground his teeth, keeping a tight rein on his surging emotions. Would this fool ever shut up?

To keep his mind occupied, he looked about the bare, little private cemetery. Hiram's grave made eight, and Harl thought with grim humor that if Ira succeeded in taking over the Bow Gun, Hiram would be nearby to haunt him.

Wilkie finally finished, and Harl nodded grudging approval. Wilkie's talk was too long and flowery, but he gave Wilkie credit for doing the best he could.

Wilkie came over to Harl after the service was over and asked anxiously, "Was it all right, Harl?"

"Just fine, Sam," Harl said and tried to make his voice hearty. "I'll be in in the morning to settle up."

"No rush," Wilkie answered. "At your convenience."

Wilkie finally left, and Cully came over and said, "Harl, why don't you take Miss Addie into the house. That wind's picking up a bit. We can finish up here."

Harl was grateful to Cully. When this man said something, he meant it. Cully and the others were taking a tremendous burden off Harl's shoulders. Filling the grave would take quite a bit of work.

"Thanks, Cully," Harl said and gripped his shoulder.

"I'll carve a tombstone tonight," Cully offered.

"That will be just fine," Harl said. Cully was a genius with a knife. Half the tombstones in this cemetery were his work.

Harl walked Addie to the house. She took off her coat and said, "I'm going to sit for a minute, Harl. I don't know why I'm so tuckered out."

Harl nodded. This kind of emotion would drain anyone.

"Harl, are you sure you won't mind waiting for supper?"

"Don't fret it, Ma. I'm not hungry anyway."

As he started to leave the room, Addie asked, "What comes now?"

"Newman's trial," he said shortly.

A wince crossed Addie's face. "I suppose there'll be a lot of washing of dirty linen."

"I'm afraid so, Ma. Whatever lawyer defends Newman will try to make Hiram look as bad as he can. He won't get

Newman off," he said with a savage rush of feelings. "He can't get Newman off, no matter what he says."

"Will you be there, Harl?"

"I'll be there," Harl said grimly. He would do anything he could to convict Newman.

When he started out of the room again, Addie asked softly, "Will this make a change between you and Melody?"

"I don't know," he replied honestly. "It could since her brother is involved."

"Ah, I hope not," Addie murmured.

Harl felt the same way. He hadn't allowed himself to think of a possible rift. "It all depends upon Melody."

"Harl," Addie said suddenly. "I want to go to that trial."

Harl turned, his face distressed. "Are you sure, Ma?" The Starks had always been a proud and aloof people. Greedy hands would try to pull them down.

"I am," Addie said firmly.

Harl sighed. He knew better than to try and talk her out of her decision. "I'll let you know when it's set, Ma," he said and left the room.

Chapter Thirteen

Andy Anderson was in Rader's office in the morning when Harl came in. Anderson was the city prosecutor, and he did better than just a competent job. He was a sleepy-eyed man, and often his face was blank, but there was a keen and facile mind behind those drowsy eyes.

"Morning, Harl," Anderson greeted him. "Quincy and I were just talking over what promises to be an interesting case."

Harl grunted. Rader hadn't lost any time moving on his investigation.

"How did the funeral go?" Rader asked.

"As well as could be expected," Harl replied. "Wilkie got wound up on one of his endless talks."

Rader clucked sympathetically, and Anderson said cynically, "One of the small prices of dying."

"How did Addie take it?" Rader asked.

"Never a buckle in her, Quincy. That lady's made of tough fiber."

"Her kind always are," Rader stated. "Harl, tell Andy what you told me about what happened at the bank."

Harl's face hardened. "Somebody tried to make it look as though Hiram tried to draw. He didn't. I saw it all."

The sleepiness was gone from Anderson's eyes. "You're positive of what you're saying."

"I am."

Anderson stared into space, then said in a musing voice, "That might change everything. Did Hiram give any indication that he might be reaching for his gun?"

Harl frowned. He wanted to be honest. "He might have. He got to coughing and reached for a handkerchief. That cold had bothered him all winter. He always carried a pocketful of handkerchiefs."

"Do you know what you're implying, Harl?" Anderson asked. "If what you say is true, then somebody planned Hiram's death all along."

"I'm not changing a word," Harl said brusquely.

"Were any words exchanged, Harl?"

"A lot of them. Hiram couldn't make a payment. After last winter—" Harl paused.

Anderson's expression became more intense. Harl thought Anderson believed him and that helped.

"Is that when the argument started?" Anderson asked.

"Just about. It really got hot when Ira said if Hiram didn't make the payment, he was going to foreclose on him."

Anderson looked startled. "Did he actually make that threat?"

"He did, Andy."

Anderson stared straight ahead, his eyes narrowed. Harl didn't break into Anderson's thoughts. He had the feeling that whatever Anderson was thinking could be important to him.

"It looks like Ira's suddenly got ambitious," Anderson said. "Maybe he's discovered an easy way to amass a chunk of Montana land. Hiring Newman is tied in to this some way."

"Have you talked to Newman yet?" Harl asked.

"Just spent an hour talking to him. He sticks to his claim that he was only doing his job. But I tell you he's scared. His voice shook every time he said, 'Hiram tried to draw. The gun lying beside him was proof of that.'"

"That's a goddamned lie," Harl said emphatically.

"I'm getting the same feeling," Anderson said. "I think he's scared of going to prison. He didn't admit it, but it's like a body odor you can smell."

"Do you think Hiram's shooting was cooked up between Temple and Newman?" Harl asked.

"I'm not prepared to say," Anderson stated. "I haven't talked to Temple yet. I think one of two things is sealing Newman's lips. Fear, or he's being paid to keep quiet."

Harl's eyes blazed. "Isn't that conspiracy?"

"You're damned right it is," Anderson said vigorously. "I'll know more after I talk to Temple. But I don't want to do that until I get him into court. There's no sense in tipping my hand this early."

Harl could reluctantly agree on that. He was glad he wasn't going to be up against this sharp mind. "When will the trial be, Andy?"

"Two weeks at least," Anderson answered. "Old Judge Hambert won't be here on his circuit until then." He misread Harl's expression. "It can't be rushed any faster, Harl."

"I know that," Harl said morosely. "But that gives Ira a lot of time to go ahead with whatever he's got in mind."

"Making that payment will block him, Harl."

"Time ran out yesterday," Harl said flatly.

Anderson whistled softly. "That makes it kinda sticky, doesn't it?"

"It does," Harl agreed flatly. "Can Ira make good on his threat?"

"Even without seeing the mortgage I'm almost certain he can. That foreclosure clause is usual bank procedure. You never ran across this before with Pike?"

Harl shook his head. "Never had to worry about it. Pike never looked for a vise he could use to squeeze anybody."

Anderson sighed. "Two different men. Ira always had illusions of grandeur. Pike kept him squeezed down. I guess Pike saw the small man in Ira." He slouched in his chair, looking almost asleep. "Maybe the trial will bring out some interesting information."

Harl's face brightened. Maybe things weren't as bleak as

he thought. "Andy, will you look into that mortgage for me?"

"Be glad to, Harl."

"Quincy, do you want me to stay around any longer? I want to go back to the ranch. A million little things to catch up." He grimaced. "Seems almost foolish to try to do them, if Ira goes through with his threat."

Rader walked to the door with him. "If I need you, I'll get in touch."

Harl nodded. "Appreciate everything you've done."

Rader's shrug was deprecatory. "Nothing yet. Wait until after the trial."

Harl walked down the street, his face thoughtful. He had left a horse at the livery stable yesterday. He'd better pick him up while he was here.

He turned a corner and almost bumped into Melody. His heart bounded at the sight of her. Lord, she grew prettier every day. Harl kept his face stolid. Before yesterday, he could state emphatically that nothing could ever come between them. Now, he wasn't so sure. It all depended upon which side she took.

"Melody," he said soberly. He saw her stiffen and guessed at the reason. This wasn't his usual warm greeting.

"Harl, I heard about yesterday. I'm so sorry."

"Thanks," he said in a frozen voice. "Who told you about it?"

Bewilderment touched her face. "Why, Ira, of course. It shook him up pretty bad."

"Did it?" Harl couldn't keep the skepticism from showing in his voice.

The stiffness increased in her. "What does that mean?"

"Nothing," he said evasively. He had said too much already. "I've got some things to do, Melody." He started to walk past her, and she reached out to detain him.

"Not until we get this straightened out, Harl. You sound like you're blaming Ira for something."

That dogged stubbornness stamped his face. "I'm in no position to say anything now, Melody. The trial might solve a few things."

Her face flushed an angry red. "You're accusing Ira, aren't you?"

Harl felt a mournful sickness steal through him. He could see the rift stretching between them, a chasm so wide that it looked unspannable. He couldn't blame her for her viewpoint. After all, Ira was her brother.

"I'll see you, Melody," he said and started forward.

"Will you?" Her voice was cold and withdrawn. The tone of the question said they'd never meet again, at least, not on friendly terms.

He walked a half block before he looked back. She still stood there, her face unyielding. Harl wanted to yell at the unfairness of life. That once bright, shining dream he had was shattered into a heap of debris. He sighed. Maybe this was another echo Hiram spoke of. It looked as though that goddamned winter would never stop sending out those echoes.

Chapter Fourteen

Ed Daniels sauntered into Rader's office. He was flamboyant in dress, and his very appearance annoyed Rader. Rader had never felt much warmth for Daniels. He admitted his cleverness as a lawyer, but he was too devious.

"What's it this time, Ed?" he asked sourly. "More dirty work for Temple?"

Daniels chuckled cheerfully. He had a thick hide that nothing could penetrate. "Just doing an honest day's work for an honest dollar," he replied.

Rader's snort expressed his doubt. "Get on with it," he snapped.

Daniels pulled some papers out of his pocket. "Mr. Temple wants you to serve this notice on Harl Stark."

"Temple doesn't waste any time, does he?"

The surliness of the remark left Daniels unperturbed. "Why should he, Quincy? That property is his now. Hiram's missed payment saw to that. You better look these papers over. You'll find the eviction notice is in order."

"You expect me to serve that?" Rader howled.

That put a cold glint in Daniels' eyes. "That's part of your job, isn't it? Do you want me to report that you refuse to serve these papers?"

Rader sighed. Daniels had him in a bind and knew it. He scanned the few papers, and the stubbornness in his shaking head grew. "This says immediate possession of the Bow Gun. Harl's got cattle out there."

"Tell him to move them," Daniels said coldly.

"I won't do it," Rader snapped. "I'll go talk to the judge

who issued these. He'll listen to reason. Temple's unpopular enough as it is. This will only make it worse."

Daniels weighed Rader's words, then gave in. Rader was absolutely right. The whole community would come down on Temple if Harl was kicked out.

"How much time do you think Harl should have, Quincy?"

"At least a couple of months."

"Ira won't stand for that, but I'll see what he says."

"You better give him some good advice this time," Rader said heatedly, "or Ira will find himself in hot water."

Daniels' eyes were narrowed as he studied Rader. He picked up the papers and tucked them in his pocket. "I'll talk to Ira and see what he says."

"Do that," Rader said, unbending.

Anderson came into Rader's office a couple of minutes after Daniels left. "I thought I saw Daniels come out of here. I didn't want to catch up with him to check."

"You did," Rader acknowledged. "He was here to serve eviction papers on Harl." Rader's face was twisted with anger. "Can he do that, Andy?"

Anderson sighed. "I'm afraid he can. I was in the bank yesterday. Temple was out, but Duncan let me look at Hiram's mortgage. That damned clause is there. Legally, the bank owns the Bow Gun, if a payment is missed. Hiram missed that payment."

He sat down at Rader's desk and put his feet up. "Don't look so mad. Maybe this will hurt Ira. If it comes out at the trial that he planned on taking over the Bow Gun, no judge will look favorably on that."

"That doesn't do Harl any good right now," Rader said savagely. "And I'm supposed to go out there and kick him off. I told Daniels I wouldn't do it, that Harl had to have time to move his cattle. I suggested two months."

"Good for you," Anderson approved. "If Ira doesn't

agree, we'll find out how he stands up under the lash of public opinion."

"I get madder every time I think of Temple," Rader growled.

Anderson chuckled. "Join the crowd, Quincy."

Addie was at the window again. She did a lot of that lately. Harl knew she wasn't looking at anything except what was locked in her mind. No one else could see those pictures.

"You better sit down, Ma," he said gently.

"I'll sit down when I want to," she said with asperity. "I was just looking out over the cemetery. I wonder if Hiram knows what's going on."

"I doubt it, Ma."

She shook her head in denial. "I'll bet he does. I'll bet he knows everything that's going on here. He loved this land so much."

That was wild talk, and it frightened Harl. He couldn't stand to see Addie losing her grip.

Addie turned from the window. "Any word from Ira?"

"No," he answered soberly.

"Maybe he'll think it over and change his mind," she suggested.

Harl grimly shook his head. That wasn't Temple's way. Once he got an idea in his head, he drove straight ahead.

Addie turned back to the window. "Somebody's coming," she announced.

Harl joined her at the window, his face drawn. He didn't know who the arrival was yet, but this was a symbol of their living from now on; dread at every visitor's appearance.

"It's Rader," he said, relief ringing in his voice. He was holding the door open by the time Rader arrived. "Come in, Quincy. Come in." Quincy was a friend.

Rader wouldn't look at either of them as he accepted the

offer. "Maybe you wouldn't invite me in, if you knew the news I'm bringing."

That dread clamped about Harl's throat again. "Say it and get it over with."

"Temple's foreclosed on you, Harl. Everything's legal. He went to a judge and got the eviction notice."

Harl wanted to swear, but Addie was here. "Did Andy check on that mortgage?" he asked wildly.

"He did, Harl. That clause was in the papers Hiram signed. There's not a damned thing you can do about it."

Harl wanted to drive his fists through something, preferably Temple.

"I did get a small extension, Harl," Rader said quickly. "Temple agreed to let you stay on here an additional two months. Daniels brought me word before I came out here. That sanctimonious bas—" He glanced at Addie and broke off. "Daniels said Temple doesn't want to push you too hard."

"I'd like to get my hands on him," Harl said bitterly.

Addie shrugged in resignation. "Don't try to fight him, Harl. With the law on his side, it could only make things worse for us."

"But what do we do, Ma?" Harl asked.

"We can start over again."

She meant that. First, there was the blow of the winter, and another more savage blow was following.

Addie saw Harl's distress. "We'll take each day as it comes, Harl, and try to save our sanity."

Harl squeezed her hand. That toughness ran all through her. She never wavered even under the most adverse conditions.

"What do you plan to do, Harl?" Rader asked.

Harl shrugged bitterly. "There isn't much choice. I can't stay here. I'm afraid Temple might come out, and I'd see him. I'm not sure what I would do. If Temple gives us a couple of months, Ma can stay here. I'm going into town."

Rader fumbled awkwardly for words. "Temple says your help can stay on here. He'll give them jobs."

"I'll tell them," Harl said gruffly. He was sure what their response would be. They wouldn't want to work for Temple.

Addie walked with Harl to the door. "Harl, have you seen Melody yet?"

Harl's face turned stiff. "I saw her."

"That bad, eh?" Addie asked knowingly.

"Our voices were getting sharp when I walked away," Harl said grimly. "All she could see was protecting her brother. To hell with everything else that got in the way."

"That's only a normal reaction, Harl."

Harl shook his head. "Not with me, it isn't. She either sticks with me, or she's against me."

"Pretty rough on her, aren't you?"

"Maybe." There was no relenting in the word. "Tell Quincy I'll be right back."

Harl's face was taut as he walked into the bunkhouse. Two of his riders lolled on their bunks, the other four were playing poker for matches. They took the game seriously, for Cully swore at a hand and threw the cards from him.

"I haven't had a decent hand in years," he said furiously. He saw Harl's expression and asked anxiously, "Something happen, Harl?"

"The worst," Harl replied. "Hiram couldn't make a payment to Temple. He was so anxious to get the money I doubt if he read what he signed. When he missed that payment, the entire amount came due."

Harl saw the slackening of faces.

"Can Temple make it stick?" Cully asked.

"He already has. Rader just rode out with the eviction notice."

His smile was strained as he listened to their swearing. They didn't overlook an oath.

"Rader also brought the news that I've got a sixty-day extension. Temple has also offered to keep all of you on."

"He knows what he can do with that offer," Cully said succinctly. "I'm not working for him."

Five other heads nodded in agreement. The swearing broke out anew, and Harl waited until it stopped.

"I'm going into town," Harl said. "I'm afraid of what I might do if I saw Ira on this land. But Addie's going to stay here for a while anyway. I'd appreciate it if you'd stay with her until I can make other arrangements."

Cully walked with Harl to the bunkhouse door. "Things will work out all right, Harl."

Harl kept his mouth shut. Anything that came out now would be bitter. Instead, he only nodded.

"We'll look after things," Cully promised.

"I'd appreciate that," Harl said gruffly.

He walked back to the house and stepped inside. Rader turned an inquiring face toward him.

"Every one of them refuses to work for Temple, Quincy. They'll stay out here with Addie until the extension is used up."

"I expected that," Rader replied. "You say you're coming into town?" At Harl's nod, he went on, "I want to see you in the morning."

Harl didn't see what Rader could do, but he said, "I'll be there, Quincy."

He saw Rader to the door, then returned to Addie. "I want to pack a few things, Ma. You'll be all right with the boys staying here."

"Things will turn out all right, Harl."

His expression said he didn't believe her.

"Is it better not to believe?" she challenged. "Without faith where would we be?"

Harl gave that a moment's thought. "Nowhere, I guess, Ma."

Chapter Fifteen

Rader and Anderson were engaged in serious talk when Harl entered Rader's office. They stopped too suddenly, and Harl said, "Talking about me, huh?"

Anderson grinned mockingly. "How did you guess? Quincy was just telling me about what happened yesterday. Looks like Temple has started his big play. Wouldn't it be funny if he got possession of the Bow Gun and couldn't get anybody to work it for him? Quincy says your boys refused to work for Temple."

Harl nodded. "That's some satisfaction, Andy, but not enough. It won't hold. Temple would have the ranch. Besides, somebody will drift by and jump at the offer of a job."

"You're right, Harl," Anderson said soberly. "I was just trying to lift your spirits."

"I've got a better idea," Rader interrupted. "How does all this leave you for money?"

Harl winced. "My pockets aren't heavy. Maybe I can stretch what I've got until after the trial."

"I've got a job open here," Rader offered. "You remember Grimson?"

Harl nodded. Everybody knew that crusty, old deputy. "You offering me his job?"

"It's open. The winter made Grimson tuck his tail between his legs and run. He's heading for south Texas. He swore he never wanted to see snow again."

"Shows more sense than most of us," Harl commented. He toyed with the idea of being a deputy. He had never worn a badge.

"It doesn't pay much," Rader said. "But it'd mean a few dollars coming in. It could ease the pinch, and you'd be a big help to me."

"You don't have to say anything more," Harl said abruptly. The job would give him something to do, and that would be more important than the money. He had dreaded the thought of hanging around town until the trial started. "When do I start?"

"How's right now suit you?"

At Harl's nod, Rader pulled a badge from a desk drawer. He stood and pinned the badge on Harl's coat. With a few words Harl was sworn in, and Rader grinned. "That badge doesn't look bad on him, does it?"

"Maybe he'll do such a good job, Quincy, it'll put the idea in voter's heads they can get a better sheriff," Anderson said.

"It's a thought," Rader grunted. "Maybe I'd better hustle around and dig up a few facts about Hiram's shooting. If it can be brought out that Temple wanted him killed, it'd make Temple back away from the Bow Gun like he touched something hot. You'd rather go back to the Bow Gun, wouldn't you, Harl?"

"And how," Harl said with fervor.

Rader grinned at Anderson. "There goes the threat to my job." A thought tightened his face. "Does making him my deputy ban him from testifying at the trial?"

Anderson pondered over the question. "Don't see why it should. He's an important witness to the shooting." He turned toward Harl, and the sleepiness was gone from his eyes. "Would you object to Addie testifying, Harl?"

The question startled Harl. "I don't see any reason why she should. She wasn't there."

"Information coming from a woman can make testimony important," Anderson said.

"What do you intend to question her about?"

Anderson shook his head. "I'm not sure. But the right moment for her to testify might come along. Thinking about it before the trial might put a strain on her. It could make her sound premeditated." Exasperation showed in his face. "Good Lord, Harl. Don't you trust me? We're both working toward the same end."

The stiffness left Harl. He had talked to Andy long enough to know Anderson was going to do his best for him.

"Sorry, Andy."

Anderson waved a forgiving hand. "No toes mashed."

Harl turned toward Rader. "You got something for me to do now, Quincy?"

"See if you can talk to Charley Duncan."

"He wasn't there when Hiram was shot," Harl protested.

"I know that. But he worked for several days with Newman. Maybe Newman let something drop. I haven't talked to Charley yet."

"Charley might talk to me," Harl said thoughtfully, "if Ira isn't there."

Rader grinned savagely at him. "Then it's up to you to pick a time when Ira isn't at the bank."

"I'll pick the right time," Harl said emphatically. He reset his hat and went out of the door. It looked as though Rader was just fishing in an empty hole, but the right bait might get a nibble. Harl knew he would do anything he could to close a noose around Temple's neck.

Chapter Sixteen

Through the bank window, Harl saw Temple talking to
Duncan. Harl moved hastily across the street. He didn't
know how long he had to wait, but there was no hope of
talking to Duncan until Temple was gone.

He waited the better part of an hour before Temple came
out of the bank. Temple's set face showed he was preoccupied with something. His head was thrust forward, his
shoulders bunched.

Harl watched him go down the street, his face cold.
Never before had he had reason to hate a man, but a deep
hatred was building up in him for Ira Temple.

He waited a few more minutes, then crossed the street.
Duncan was absorbed in some work, and he didn't look up
until Harl said, "Hello, Charley."

Did Duncan flinch, or was that imagination?

Duncan's face looked strained. "Did you want to see Ira,
Harl? He's out right now."

"I saw him leave, Charley. I want to talk to you."

That could be a harried flash in Duncan's eyes. "What
about, Harl?"

"Do you know anything about Hiram's shooting?"

Duncan ducked his head as though he wanted to avoid
meeting Harl's eyes.

"You know I don't. I wasn't even there," he said stiffly.

"I know you weren't, Charley. I want to know about
Newman. Did he say anything about Hiram before we came
in that day?"

Duncan had a tight, pinched look about his lips. "I only work here, Harl. I don't know anything."

"I was hoping you did, Charley," Harl said gravely. "We've been friends for a lot of years. I always thought of you as a man who spoke his mind regardless of the circumstances."

A hollow groan escaped Duncan. "Harl, I'm trying to avoid taking sides," he said earnestly. "But I didn't like what was going on here. Newman talked about Hiram several times. He kept asking me about Hiram's temper. Said he was going to do everything he could to protect Ira. He kept boasting that was his job."

Harl's eyes gleamed. "Would you say that at Newman's trial?"

Duncan groaned again. "That'd cost me my job, Harl. You know Ira won't stand for anybody crossing him."

"Hiram was a good friend, too," Harl said softly.

Duncan's sigh was a long, tearing sound. "I know. It's been tearing me apart. Oh, what the hell," he said half angrily. "Ira and I are bound to tangle. He's gotten more testy every passing day. I can't take much more of that." He looked squarely at Harl for the first time. "I'll testify to what I know."

Harl grabbed his hand and wrung it. "That takes a lot of guts, Charley. I don't know of many men who would—"

"Will you get out of here?" Duncan yelped. "You're putting me so far behind in my work that Ira will fire me before I expect it."

"Maybe I can show my appreciation some day," Harl said.

Duncan grimaced and pointed at the front door.

Harl grinned at him and walked toward the door. He looked back, clasped his hands, and shook them. Duncan only nodded.

Harl was thoughtful as he walked down the street. As old

as Duncan was, it would take a lot of guts to get up and say anything damaging about Temple. He was finding out there were a lot of solid people in this town: Rader, Anderson, and now Duncan.

He looked up, and Melody was just crossing the street. Her head was down, and she seemed lost in deep thought. Her eyes lifted, and she saw him. Harl saw the start that ran through her. Her mouth opened in a soundless Oh, and red flooded her face. She quickened her pace, heading toward the bank.

Harl muttered a soft oath and picked up his pace. What was done was done, and he could do nothing to recall or change it. How long did a sense of loss stay with a man? Did it gradually get worse until he was overwhelmed, or did it slowly fade until he forgot all about it? He gave the latter thought no credence. He would never forget Melody.

He walked into Rader's office and sat down. "I talked to Charley."

Rader grunted. "The important thing is did he talk to you?"

Harl nodded. "He didn't want to, but I played on an old friendship. Newman asked questions about Hiram's temper. He seemed worried about the possible chance of violence. Charley will testify at the trial."

Rader took a deep breath. "It might help, Harl. I'll tell Anderson about it. Maybe Temple and Newman are tied up in this together."

Harl's face clouded at the mention of Temple's name.

"Does hating him so much make you look that sour?" Rader asked.

"I wasn't thinking of him, Quincy. I saw Melody a moment ago. She ducked her head to avoid speaking to me."

"That's only natural," Rader said quickly. "She'd stick with her brother. Maybe the truth will come out at the trial, and she'll change her outlook."

Harl remembered the shock stamped on Melody's face. "No," he said despondently. "She'll never change."

"If she's that bullheaded, you're better off without her," Rader said sagely. He saw the stubbornness on Harl's face. Harl wouldn't believe that, but then he was young. Rader sat in silence. It was all too bad. Melody was an attractive woman, and Harl had too many blows this year to add the loss of Melody. There was nothing he could say that would soften Harl's mental attitude. Only one thing would do that, and that was time.

Rader wanted to get that bitter look off Harl's face. "Newman had a visitor while you were out."

Harl tightened at just the mention of Newman.

"Temple was in to talk to him. He demanded I leave them alone." Rader shrugged. "I could have refused, but that wouldn't have solved anything. When I looked back, they had their heads together, like they were cooking up something."

The news hadn't wiped the despondency from Harl's face, but at least, he was interested. He had something else besides his personal troubles to occupy his mind.

"I saw Temple leave the bank, Quincy. He must have headed straight here. Didn't you hear anything?"

"I told you I didn't listen. I'd sure like to know what those two talked about," Rader said slowly.

"Two of us, Quincy," Harl growled.

"Evidently, that little talk didn't go well between them. Twice, I heard them yelling at each other clear out here. When Ira came out, his face was red, and his teeth were clenched. Something went sour between them."

He leaned back in his chair and hooked his heels over the desk's edge. He looked so lazily indolent a casual observer wouldn't have guessed that Rader had a thing on his mind.

"Quincy, is there anything more I can do?" Harl asked. "Anything I can do to make the trial go smoother."

Rader grinned. "You mean go our way? Not a thing, Harl. All we can do is wait and hope something comes out in the testimony."

Harl sighed. He wished he could sprawl as thoroughly relaxed as Quincy. Waiting was always difficult for him.

Chapter Seventeen

Rader came in after making a round of the town.

Harl asked about the smug look on Rader's face.

"The waiting's about over," Rader replied. "Judge Hambert came in on the afternoon stage."

"Did you get a chance to talk to him, Quincy?"

"No, and I wasn't seeking one. The judge is a testy man, particularly after a stage trip. He also has a highly suspicious mind. If a lawman or a lawyer approaches him before a trial, he jumps to the conclusion they're trying to fix things. The smartest thing I could do was to let him alone and hope his evening meal sits well on his stomach."

"He's that tough, huh?"

"Multiply that about four times, and you come close. When he thinks somebody is trying to butter him up, he's got a temper like a rattlesnake. A lot of inexperienced lawyers have learned that to their sorrow."

Rader sat down and rolled a cigarette. "Wouldn't be surprised to see Temple pop in here any minute now. He'll want to tell Newman the judge is here."

Harl shook his head in disagreement. "Maybe not. I think he'll stay as far away as he can from Newman."

Rader whistled in appreciation. "You've got a quick mind. That could be. I thought desperation might drive Temple back here." He spread his hands and shrugged. "We'll just have to wait and see how it goes. I'd better go out and get Newman some supper."

"I can do it," Harl offered.

"Don't want to learn to depend on you too much, Harl."
Rader grinned. "It'd soften me up."

Rader came back in a half hour with a cloth-covered tray.
"Hope he likes this," he said. "Newman's been complaining
a lot lately."

"Doesn't his kind always complain?" Harl asked.

"Nearly always," Rader agreed.

Rader came back from Newman's cell without the tray,
his face angry. "Newman refused to eat. He demanded to
see Temple. He cussed me out good when I said I couldn't
do anything about that. I left the tray on his bunk. I don't
give a damn what he does with it."

"Why do you suppose he wants to see Temple, Quincy?"

"If I could answer that, I could tell you how the trial will
go tomorrow. I'll tell you one thing. The closer the trial gets
the more terrified Newman is. I've watched it grow on him
all week."

"I agree with Newman on one thing," Harl remarked.
"I'll be damned glad when it's over."

"A lot of people will. I hear Daniels is going to defend
Newman."

"Is this Daniels any good?"

"He's the lawyer who got Newman off on that first shooting a year ago. Judge Hambert wasn't too happy over the
jury's verdict. Daniels did a hell of a job. He made that
shooting sound like self-defense. That's what convinced the
jury."

"You didn't like the verdict?"

Rader shrugged. "I never argue with a verdict already in.
Waste of time."

Harl's thoughts were in a swirl. He didn't want to see
Newman get off again. He wanted his father's murderer
punished.

"Why don't you turn in, Harl? Big day tomorrow."

"What are you going to do?"

"I'll stay here tonight. I've slept many an hour in this office. Go on. I mean it."

Harl turned at the door. "I'm going back to the ranch. I want to drive Ma in. Good night, Quincy."

"No need to rush, Harl. Trial doesn't begin until nine o'clock. Sleep as well as you can."

Harl nodded soberly. With everything on his mind sleep might not come easily.

Addie was silent all during breakfast. Harl hadn't told her about Anderson calling her as a witness. It was going to be a surprise, especially to her. Harl wondered uneasily how she would take it.

He hitched the old mare to the buggy, helped Addie into her seat, and drove into town. Even as early as they arrived, people were streaming into the building where the trial was to be held.

Anderson waved to them as they entered the courtroom. He pointed to two chairs near the front of the room.

Addie's bright eyes surveyed the room. "Going to be a big crowd, isn't it?"

Harl nodded. "Big trial." Hiram was well known. And Ira certainly was, if only for Pike's reputation.

Addie scanned the jury. "I see a few on that jury are as near to being friends of Hiram as anybody could be."

Harl nodded absently. He wanted to caution her not to get her hopes too high from that fact. It wasn't any guarantee that Newman would be found guilty.

Newman sat at one of the small tables in front of the bench, talking to Daniels. Daniels' and Newman's heads were close together, and Harl supposed Daniels was giving Newman some last-minute instructions.

Harl felt his gorge rise as he watched them. Daniels fancied himself invincible. It showed in every movement he made. He wore his hair inordinately long, and he kept tossing his head, or smoothing his hair back with his hand. He was too well dressed, for Harl's taste, and Harl would like nothing better than to see that aristocratic nose rubbed in the dirt.

He forced himself to look away from the pair. He hadn't realized he had so much animosity in his system.

Temple sat directly behind Newman's table. He stared straight ahead, his face frozen. Harl jerked his eyes from Temple to keep his temper from showing in his face. He prayed that this trial proved that Temple and Newman were involved in some conspiracy; then maybe Temple would lose his grip on the Bow Gun.

That was rushing things, he counseled himself. He stumbled over one fact every time he came to it; he hadn't been able to make that payment. Legally, the ranch belonged to Temple, and Harl couldn't see any way to alter that.

Harl looked around to smother the dislike for Temple that pulsed up in steady waves. He saw Melody come in, her face tight and drawn. He couldn't stop the familiar clutch of a brutal hand at his guts. She was so lovely and so very far away. Sure, she was here to see her brother exonerated. Temple had lied to her when he denied all part of complicity in this mess.

The bailiff stood and intoned, "Everybody stand. The judge is coming in."

Judge Hambert came in through a rear door, looking dumpy in the worn, black robe. His face was set in severe lines, and Harl thought, Oh, oh, he didn't have a smooth night. Somebody in this room would pay for that lack of rest.

Judge Hambert let the spectators stand a moment longer than necessary before he said, "Be seated."

Harl heard body movement and the scrape of chairs as everybody sat down. That was a pitiless face up there on the bench. Harl knew that if he were in Newman's boots he would be scared to death.

"What do we have here, bailiff?" Hambert asked.

The bailiff looked at a piece of paper he held. "The next case, your honor, is the County of Custer against Mungo Newman. The charge is murdering Hiram Stark."

Hambert's harrump sounded pleased. He was always at his vicious best when he judged a murder case. He turned a stony face toward Daniels. "How does the defendant plead?"

Daniels bounded to his feet and adjusted his coat lapels. He looked about as though he wanted to make sure he had everyone's attention. He cleared his throat and said in ringing tones, "Not guilty, your honor. We are prepared to prove—"

Hambert cut him short with a wave of his hand. "That remains to be seen, Mr. Daniels," he said severely. He stopped, his mouth drooping as a thought suddenly hit him. He pointed an accusing finger at Daniels. "You handled the same charge for the same defendant last year."

Daniels bobbed his head. "Yes, sir," he said silkily. "I'm glad you remember. In that case I proved Mr. Newman was wrongly charged. I proved—"

Hambert held up his hand. "I don't need to listen to your self-laudatory palaver. Just get on to the facts."

All the vigor left Daniels' nod. "Yes, sir," he said meekly. His face was red, and he looked crushed.

Hambert turned to Anderson. "Mr. Anderson will you call your first witness?"

"Yes, sir. I call as my first witness Mungo Newman."

That pulled a gasp of surprise from the watching people. Nobody had expected Newman to be called first. The jurors craned their necks and whispered among themselves.

Hambert banged away with his gavel. "Order, order," he bawled. "Any more of this disgraceful conduct, and I'll clear the court."

The audience knew he would, too, for immediate silence fell on the room. Daniels was on his feet spluttering objections.

"What are your objections precisely?" Hambert asked sternly.

Daniels gesticulated wildly. "Mr. Newman is my client. Mr. Anderson has no right—"

"If it pleases your honor," Anderson interrupted, "why shouldn't Mr. Newman be my witness, too. He saw everything that happened in that room. I'm questioning him first in the hope of speeding up this case."

Hambert appeared pleased as he looked at Anderson. "About time somebody feels that way. Objection overruled. Proceed, Mr. Anderson."

Mungo Newman approached the witness chair and sat down. He was visibly disturbed, for his eyes rolled and his lips trembled.

Daniels showed agitation, and Harl thought maybe Anderson had upset Daniels' order of things by calling Newman first.

The bailiff swore Newman in, and Anderson glided toward him. His eyes were on the floor. He appeared to be more interested in what he saw there, than in Newman.

"State your name," Anderson said almost pleasantly.

"Mungo Newman." His voice was so low that even Harl, sitting so near, barely heard it.

"Louder," Anderson said. "I don't believe the jurors heard you."

Newman repeated his name and apprehensively watched the attacking lawyer.

"How long have you resided in Miles City, Mr. Newman?"

"Six years," Newman replied.

"Have you been in trouble before?" The question was deceptively soft.

Newman cast harried eyes at Daniels, and its message was plain to everyone. Newman needed advice.

Daniels was on his feet, protesting. "That isn't germane to this case, your honor. I know you are interested only in this current case."

"Will you let me be the judge of that?" Hambert snapped. "Proceed, Mr. Anderson."

"Mr. Newman, you haven't answered my question," Anderson purred.

Newman pulled at his fingers, and the sound of the popping knuckles could plainly be heard. He gulped and said, "Yes, sir. I was in trouble before. It was a clear case of self-defense. The judge can vouch for that."

"Just answer the question, Mr. Newman," Hambert said in evident disgust.

Newman was breathing harder, and his head was lowered as though it were suddenly too heavy to support. "I was in trouble before," he said sullenly.

The silkiness in Anderson's voice increased. "Practically the same trouble before, wasn't it, Mr. Newman?"

Rader turned his head and looked at Harl. He gave Harl a brief wink. The wink said, Anderson was tearing Newman to pieces.

Newman took a long time before he answered.

"Never mind," Anderson said as though suddenly weary at the trend this was taking. "How long have you been working for Mr. Temple?"

Harl noticed the question made Temple stiffen. Was Temple afraid of what Newman might say?

"Two weeks," Newman replied, his face sullen.

Anderson evinced surprise. "Only two weeks. That wasn't very long before you ran into trouble again, was it? Why did Mr. Temple hire you? You had no experience at being a bank guard, did you?"

"I knew what to expect."

"What did you expect?" Anderson shot the question at Newman.

"I knew Hiram Stark's reputation. He was a hot-tempered man. If he lost his head, he could shoot Mr. Temple. It almost happened."

Anderson paced absently for a moment, then whirled on

Newman. Beside Newman's bulk, he looked like a feisty terrier.

"Did Mr. Temple tell you that?"

Harl could swear Temple's face turned ashen, and it looked as though he stopped breathing while he awaited the answer.

"No, sir," Newman said vigorously. "He did not. I just heard it various places about town."

Temple looked on the verge of collapse.

Anderson went back to his attack. "Tell us where some of those various places are."

Newman's face twisted as he sought for plausible answers. He panted and squirmed as he labored to come up with an answer.

"It's apparent that you can't name those places right off hand," Anderson said relentlessly. "Then tell us about the morning of the shooting from the time Mr. Stark came into the bank."

"He was in a bad mood when he came in," Newman answered cautiously. "It stuck out all over him. Anybody could see that he was primed for trouble."

"Did anybody else notice his mood?" Anderson asked. He watched Newman struggle for an answer, then said impatiently, "Forget it. Tell us about the actual shooting."

"Mr. Stark and his son came in. After a few words with Charley Duncan, they headed for Mr. Temple's office. I followed them there. That was part of my job. As security guard, I was supposed to see that nothing happened to Mr. Temple, or to any of the bank's property."

Harl caught the ghastly pallor of Temple's face and thought, He's really scared of something.

"Did you just decide to shoot Mr. Stark because you thought he looked dangerous?"

"I wouldn't do that," Newman said stubbornly. "But he kept getting madder and madder. I didn't do anything until he grabbed for his gun."

"You saw him grab for his gun?" Anderson asked in mock astonishment.

"I sure did. It was in his hip pocket. He almost beat me. The gun was in his hand before I shot. He fell and dropped it."

Harl ground his teeth to keep from yelling out, "You damned liar." Maybe Anderson knew what he was doing, but it seemed as though the testimony were going in favor of Newman.

"So you saw him draw and shot him," Anderson said musingly.

"What else could I do?" Newman pleaded. "Mr. Temple was in danger."

Anderson suddenly thrust his face close to Newman's. "You know what will happen to you if it's proven you're lying? You can hang."

"Objection," Daniels bellowed, bouncing to his feet. "He is threatening the witness."

"Sustained," Hambert said frostily. "You know better than that."

Anderson smiled. "I do, your honor." He faced Newman again. "Do you wish to change your story? Telling the truth could make it easier."

"Objection," Daniels roared. He looked beside himself. "Despite your warning, your honor, my opponent is doing it again."

Hambert leaned forward as though he wished to get closer to Anderson. "I won't warn you again, Mr. Anderson."

Anderson nodded weakly. "I promise it won't happen again."

He refaced Newman. "You say he reached for his hip pocket?"

Newman nodded.

"That's odd," Anderson mused. "Mr. Stark was wearing a holstered gun."

"That's the way it looked to me," Newman mumbled.

"Mr. Stark was shot in the back," Anderson went on relentlessly. "There was no real danger to you."

"I knew he was drawing on Mr. Temple," Newman protested. "I was protecting him." He looked up at Hambert. "Judge, could I say something?" Newman's eyes seemed to bulge from his face. "I didn't want to shoot Mr. Stark. But he kept getting madder and madder. I didn't do anything until he grabbed for his gun."

"You insist on that hard-to-believe story?" Anderson sneered.

"I sure do. He jerked it out of the holster, and I shot then."

He looked fearfully at Judge Hambert. "I didn't want to do it. But he was threatening Mr. Temple. I couldn't allow that. Mr. Temple was good to me. He gave me a job when I'd been out of work for a long time."

Hambert wearily shook his head. "I don't see where all this self-justification is getting us, Mr. Anderson."

"I'm finished with this witness, your honor."

"Then for God's sake, get rid of him."

Anderson dismissed Newman. "I call Mrs. Addie Stark as my next witness."

Harl knew it was coming, but still it startled him. He watched Addie take the witness chair.

"Don't be nervous, Mrs. Stark," Anderson said gently. "I just want to ask a couple of questions."

"Who's nervous?" Addie asked in disdain.

"Would you say, Mrs. Stark, that you knew Hiram Stark well?"

"I should," she snapped. "I lived with him for forty years. If a woman doesn't know a man in that time, she isn't trying, or is simply not interested."

Anderson hid his smile. "Would you say that Hiram was a violent man?"

She considered that question. "I don't know what you mean."

"Would Hiram kill a man?"

Addie pondered over that question, then violently shook her head. "In all that forty years, he never killed anybody. If you don't count the Indians. I know all about his temper. I'd seen enough of it. He was often mad enough to hit a man." Again, she shook her head. "But kill him. No!"

"You don't think he'd try to shoot Mr. Temple."

"He would not," she said positively. "Oh, he probably would get mad enough to cuss him out, and he might try to beat Mr. Temple with his fists, but he wouldn't attempt to kill him. I wasn't there to see what happened, but Harl told me—"

"That's all, Mrs. Stark," Anderson said hastily. "We will listen to Harl's story later. I'm through, your honor."

"Do you want to question the witness, Mr. Daniels?" Hambert asked.

"I certainly do," Daniels replied. He stood, readjusted his lapels and strutted toward Addie.

Harl watched him with no worry. Daniels was walking into a buzz saw, though he didn't know it yet.

"I find it hard to believe, Mrs. Stark, that with that noted temper Mr. Stark never killed."

"Hiram never saw any occasion to kill."

"How can you be so positive, Mrs. Stark. A man would want something like that hidden from his wife."

Anderson was on his feet, protesting. "Your honor, the counselor is inferring that Mrs. Stark is a liar."

Hambert looked bleakly at Daniels. "I suggest you drop this line of questioning."

"But, your honor, it is hard for me to believe that Mr. Stark wouldn't protect his ranch if it were threatened."

Addie's chin jutted forward. "Are you calling me a liar?"

"Heaven forbid," Daniels said, appalled. "I certainly wouldn't want to give that impression." He gave her a confident smile. "If the circumstances were just right, how can you say Hiram would never kill?"

"Because I knew him," she snapped. "What would those circumstances be?"

A flush crept up Daniels' neck. "If he faced the danger of losing his ranch—" He stopped, realizing he was saying too much.

"You're talking about the bank, aren't you? As long as Pike had the bank, Hiram never had to fear that."

Anderson stood. "Counselor is badgering the witness."

Hambert's expression was stern. "My opinion exactly. Mr. Daniels, I suggest you drop this line of questioning, or change to another subject."

Daniels looked helplessly about him. His eyes swept across Temple, and he gulped. "I guess I'm finished with this witness, your honor."

Addie sniffed as she stepped down. Her head was carried high as she walked to her chair.

Anderson was visibly delighted.

Harl squeezed Addie's hand as she sat down beside him. She had done just fine.

"I call Harl Stark as my next witness," Anderson announced.

Daniels objected violently, and Anderson asked smoothly, "On what grounds? Harl walked into the bank with Mr. Stark. He was there until the finish."

"Harl is a prejudiced witness," Daniels said feebly.

"Overruled," Hambert announced. "Go ahead, Mr. Anderson."

Harl took the witness chair, and Anderson said easily, "Tell your story in your own words, Harl."

Harl appreciated that Anderson was setting this up so he could talk with no interruptions.

"I rode into town with Pa. He had his gun with him. After twenty years of carrying it, it was a hard-to-break habit. I'll admit he reached for his hip pocket. What he had in there was a wad of handkerchiefs. He needed them. He had a bad cold. It hung on all winter. Twice on the way, he had to use a handkerchief. Just keeping them clean was a chore for Ma." He smiled at her and received a fleeting one in return.

Daniels got to his feet. "I don't see where any of this trivia has anything—"

"If my learned opponent will only give the witness a chance to go on," Anderson said blandly.

Daniels sat down under Hambert's fierce gaze.

"We came in to see Mr. Temple about an extension of our loan," Harl went on. "If Pike Temple had been alive, we wouldn't have had the slightest trouble. Pike was always patient with a rancher struggling through a bad time. God knows, last winter was that."

Daniels was on his feet again. "Irrelevant," he shouted.

Hambert nodded. "Granted. Mr. Anderson, tell your witness to refer only to facts that are pertinent."

"Yes, sir. Harl, tell only what happened."

Harl nodded. "Newman followed us into Temple's office. We wondered about that, and Hiram squawked a little. Temple said it was to protect the bank. Hiram quieted down and asked for an extension of his loan. Even before he got his request out of his mouth, Temple was shaking his head. I'll admit that made Hiram mad. I could see it in his face. He started to say something and choked up. That was when he reached for his handkerchief. He wanted to clear his throat. Newman picked that moment to shoot him." Harl's face twisted at the memory.

"Is that all, Harl?" Anderson asked gently.

"No, sir," Harl replied in a low voice. "I tried to get at Newman. He hit me with his gun barrel, knocking me cold. I don't know what happened until I came to, and Rader was in the room."

"Then you don't think Hiram was reaching for a gun," Anderson persisted.

"I know he wasn't," Harl said firmly. "His gun was still in his holster when he fell."

"But Mr. Newman testified that the gun was lying beside Hiram," Anderson said. He turned to Daniels. "Your witness, Counselor."

Daniels moved toward Harl, his face truculent. "Are you suggesting that somebody placed the gun beside Hiram while you were unconscious?"

"It's your suggestion, sir," Harl said levelly.

Daniels' mistake in judgment showed in his blinking eyes. He tried to recover and sneered. "It seems to me you're trying to make a mystery of how that gun got out of its holster."

"You're trying to keep it a mystery," Harl shot back. "The gun wasn't in Hiram's hand when he fell. There were only four people in that room. Hiram was dead, and I was unconscious."

"Are you accusing Mr. Temple or Mr. Newman of pulling that gun out of your father's holster and placing it beside him?"

Harl grinned. He was finding enjoyment in this encounter. "Again, it's your suggestion, sir."

Daniels stopped, nonplused. Hambert broke up the moment by saying, "Are you going to stand there all day?"

Anderson winked at Harl, and Harl stepped down. "I call Sheriff Rader to the stand," Anderson called.

Rader was an old hand at this, and no pressure could wilt him.

He sat down and said, "I found Hiram dead and Harl just recovering. I saw the gun, lying near Hiram's body." The distaste in his voice showed what he thought of all this.

"Did you search the body, Sheriff?"

Rader nodded. "I found a hip pocket stuffed with handkerchiefs, just as Harl said. Maybe as Harl said, Hiram was reaching for his hip pocket and not his gun."

"Go on," Anderson prompted.

"I arrested Newman and held him for trial. He admitted the shooting, but he called it self-defense."

Anderson turned those sleepy eyes on Newman. He looked back at Rader. "Would you think that might be an excuse to get out of a stupid mistake?"

Daniels bounded to his feet, howling his objections. "That asks the witness for an opinion."

Hambert banged him quiet. "Maybe this case needs a fresh opinion. Objection overruled. The witness can answer the question."

"I sure do," Rader drawled.

"That'll do," Anderson said. "Your witness."

Daniels didn't want any part of Rader. He had had experience with Rader before.

"I call Mr. Temple," Anderson said.

He stared at Temple until Temple took the witness chair. Anderson's face was stern. All vestige of sleepiness had vanished from his eyes. "Was there an argument with Mr. Stark?"

"Yes," Temple said in a voice so low that it was almost inaudible.

"You'll have to speak louder," Anderson instructed him. "I doubt if the judge heard you."

Hambert nodded his appreciation. "Mr. Temple, you will speak louder," he said firmly.

Temple nodded dumbly. He looked ill.

"Did you tell your guard to anticipate trouble with Mr. Stark?"

"I don't think so," Temple mumbled.

"Then why did he follow Harl and Hiram into your office?"

"He was only doing his job," Temple replied. His eyes wandered all over the room. "He knew he was supposed to stop trouble."

"Ah," Anderson murmured and asked quietly, "Why did you hire him in the first place? He had no experience in this kind of work."

Harl enjoyed seeing Temple squirm. Bleed, he thought viciously.

"I was fearful for my safety," Temple said.

Anderson looked astounded. "From whom?"

"From Hiram Stark. His temper was well known. He had a payment due. I didn't expect him to make it."

"How could you assume such a thing?" Anderson asked softly.

Temple shrugged. "After the bad winter, nobody had any money."

"Did Hiram react as you expected him to?" Anderson asked.

"He lost his head, if that's what you mean."

"Exactly what did you say that made him lose his temper?"

Temple looked furtively about him. He didn't want to answer. "I told him he was in danger of losing his ranch."

"More than danger," Anderson said grimly. "Isn't it true you've already served eviction notice on Harl?"

"What else could I do?" Temple pleaded. "A bank can't be run on missed payments."

"The shock of hearing he could lose his ranch put Hiram into a coughing spell, Mr. Temple. He reached for his handkerchief, and your guard, mistaking the motion, shot him," Anderson hammered at him.

"That's not true," Temple shouted.

Anderson looked at the judge. "It looks to me as though there was some kind of a conspiracy in this matter."

Daniels jumped to his feet, hollering his head off. "Your honor, my opponent is accusing Mr. Temple without basis of any kind. I request he should be instructed to stop it."

"Some of Mr. Anderson's sentiments come close to my own," Hambert said coldly. "Are you finished with the witness, Mr. Anderson?"

"I think I've heard all I need," Anderson replied.

Temple's legs seemed to be melting under him as he made

his way back to his seat. Harl turned his head to watch him.
He saw Melody stare at her brother, her face still and white.

Harl thought in exultation, her suspicions are aroused,
too.

"Any more witnesses?" Judge Hambert asked.

"One more, sir. I call Charley Duncan."

Duncan's face was grim as he took the chair. He gave his
name and occupation in a grumpy tone.

"Mr. Duncan," Anderson said, "I want you to tell all you
know about this."

"I ain't lying for nobody," Duncan said indignantly.

"Do you know why Mr. Temple hired Newman?"

"He didn't tell me," Duncan replied. "But it came right
after Mr. Temple had trouble with John Brinker and Ben
Hammond. He foreclosed on both of their ranches when
they couldn't meet a payment. Both of them screamed a lot
at him. I didn't hear the words. I was working in my cage.
But I could hear all the yelling."

"Do you think either of those two men could have turned
violent?"

Duncan thoughtfully rubbed his chin. "I can't say that.
But I can say Brinker was furious when he came out."

"Do you think it possible that he may have shot Mr. Temple, if he had a weapon with him?"

Daniels bellowed his usual objections.

"On what basis?" Hambert asked coldly.

"Mr. Anderson is asking for a pure conjecture from the
witness."

"It's an interesting question," Hambert said flatly. "I'm
curious as to the answer myself. The witness may proceed."

"He may have," Duncan admitted. "A man's driven to
some violent things when he loses his land."

"When was Newman hired?"

Duncan reflected on that question. "If I remember right,
the day after. Not more than a couple of days."

"Did you approve of the new employee?"

"I didn't see any reason why the bank needed a guard," Duncan snorted in disgust. "In all the years I worked there, we didn't need one."

"Did you talk with the new guard?"

"Several times."

"Did you like him?"

"No," Duncan said with candor. "I didn't see him doing any work that justified his pay." He smiled twistedly. "But that was none of my business."

"That's all right," Anderson said cordially. "After talking to Mr. Newman, what was your real opinion of him?"

Daniels slowly sank back into his chair. Hambert's icy eyes had forestalled his objection.

"He asked me too many damned questions about Hiram Stark," Duncan replied. "He was curious about Hiram's reported temper. He knew Hiram all right, but he wanted me to be sure and point him out when he came in."

"Did you?"

Duncan shook his head. "I got busy and didn't notice Hiram and Harl until they were right in front of my cage. I told them Ira was in, and they turned toward Mr. Temple's office. Mr. Newman followed them into Ira's office. I started to yell at him, but again, I figured it was none of my business."

"That will do, Charley. Thank you."

Duncan stepped down from the chair. He looked old and frail, but his dignity hadn't been ruffled. He glanced at Temple before he moved away.

Temple didn't say a word, but he glared at Duncan, and his stabbing finger said it all. Duncan had just lost his job.

"My last witness, your honor," Anderson said. "I believe the judge and the jurors have heard all they need."

Hambert stared at him a long, vibrant minute, then looked at the jurors. "Before you retire to reach your verdict, I'd like to make a few remarks about this case. You jurors have heard the defense witnesses and summation. It has some odd and interesting aspects. I think you heard the defense attorney do his best to establish this as a case of self-defense. My belief is that he failed. However, it is up to you gentlemen to arrive at a fair and just verdict. You can retire now."

He stood and stalked through a rear door.

Anderson came over and stood beside Harl. "What do you think, Harl?"

Harl shook his head. "I don't have enough experience to even make a guess. What do you think?"

"I think it looks good, Harl. Somebody will be found guilty of shooting Hiram. But it won't be Temple. I wonder what made Newman keep his mouth shut. I thought sure he'd crumple under all that pressure," he sighed. "But he didn't buckle. He'll be convicted. That should bring you some satisfaction."

"It will, Andy. I appreciate the job you've done."

Anderson grinned. "Daniels got sucked into this mess, and the farther he went, the more he was made to look like a fool. Do you want to see if your ma would like to go out for a bite? I have no idea how long the jury will be out. I've seen some of them take a long time, and others return so fast it can take your breath."

"I'll ask her, Andy."

Addie shook her head. "I don't care how long it takes. I'm staying."

Harl had known that adamant streak before. He settled down beside her. "We'll wait together, Ma."

Chapter Eighteen

Two hours passed before the jury returned. Hambert looked at them speculatively then asked, "Have you reached your verdict?"

"We have, your honor."

"Bailiff, the verdict please," Hambert said. He sounded impatient to end this trial as though it had already taken too long.

He read the verdict the bailiff handed him, then stared at Newman and his lawyer. His mouth was tight and pinched.

"The jury finds the defendant guilty," Hambert announced.

Newman's squall sounded as though it were yanked out of him. "It's not fair," he yelled. "I was only doing my job."

Hambert pounded with his gavel. "Mr. Daniels, I advise you to keep your client quiet. The sentence could be worse. He could have been facing a premeditated murder charge. That could mean hanging. As it is, I am sentencing him to five years in the penitentiary."

A shudder ran through Newman, and he buried his face in his hands.

Good, Harl thought. He felt not the slightest pity for the man. By Newman's shaking shoulders, Harl could swear he was sobbing.

Temple looked as though he had seen a ghost. He suddenly stood, clapped his hat on his head, and plunged toward the entrance, his eyes unseeing. Harl couldn't help but notice Melody's reaction. She looked after her brother as though this were the first time she had actually seen him.

Harl turned his head to look at Rader. "Want me to go with you, Quincy?"

"What for?" Rader asked in mild surprise.

"To help you take Newman back to jail."

That did surprise Rader. "Hell, I don't need any help with him. Take your ma back to the ranch."

Harl wasn't satisfied yet. "How long do you think Newman will be around here?"

Rader thoughtfully pulled at an ear lobe. "It'll take a few days for the necessary paper work. Then the tumbleweed wagon has to have time to get here."

Harl shuddered. He could visualize himself riding in the dreadful wagon that took prisoners to the penitentiary. My God, he thought, If I faced what Newman faces, I'd go out of my head.

He turned in time to see a shabbily dressed woman rush up to Newman and fling her arms about him. Her sobs carried throughout the courtroom.

Rader gently disengaged her arms. "Here now, Mrs. Newman," he remonstrated gently, "I've got to take him now."

So that was Mrs. Newman. Harl had never seen her before. He knew a sweeping pity for her. Wasn't it always this way? The man's crime required punishment, but the woman took the brunt.

Rader finally pulled her away from Newman, and he nodded abruptly for Daniels to restrain her. Harl had never looked at a wilder expression than Newman's. He looked like an animal with a pack of hounds closing in on him.

Rader took a wise precaution. He handcuffed Newman before he took him out on the street. Harl thoroughly approved of the measure. Newman could be driven to desperation by his harried thoughts. There was no telling what he might attempt to do. If he were free, he might try to break and run. The handcuffs prevented Rader from facing the necessity of having to shoot him.

The courtroom slowly emptied. Little groups of people

stopped outside the door, talking over the day's events. This happening would furnish subject matter for many days.

Harl thought briefly about Judge Hambert. His job had to be done, but Harl wouldn't want it. There was too much room for error, and the thought of those errors could drive a man crazy.

He took Addie's arm. She looked suddenly beaten, and he asked gently, "Does this satisfy you, Ma?"

"It doesn't change anything that's been done," she said dispiritedly. "It doesn't get the Bow Gun back. Tomorrow, we'll be facing the same bleak prospect."

It was too true. Harl couldn't think of a single thing to say to lift her spirits. "We'll just take it one day at a time, Ma." His grip on her arm tightened.

Chapter Nineteen

Anderson walked with Rader back to the jail, Newman between them. Newman shuffled along, his head hanging low, keeping up a constant stream of mutterings.

Anderson listened a moment, then said, "I can't make out what he's saying."

"Me neither," Rader replied. He looked curiously at the spittle stringing down from Newman's lip corners. "Damned if he doesn't look like he's cracking up." Unconsciously, he shivered. Seeing a man lose his faculties was a frightening thing.

"I'm just as glad you're with me, Andy," he confessed.

Anderson looked anxious. "Do you expect trouble, Quincy?"

"You never know," Rader said dubiously. "The only trouble I might have with him is taking the cuffs off. He might decide to make a break then."

Newman walked along never stopping that muttering. He showed no awareness of Rader and Anderson's conversation.

Rader pushed Newman through the cell door and propelled him toward the far wall. His face turned grimmer. There was more resistance in Newman.

Rader handed his gun to Anderson. "Keep this trained on him. He might make his effort about now." He swore softly. "Jesus! Look at his eyes roll."

Rader stepped in behind Newman. "Turn around, Newman," he ordered, "so I can unlock those cuffs."

Newman's turn started slowly enough, then picked up speed. He whirled, swinging his cuffed hands at Rader.

They struck Rader across the head, knocking him against a wall.

"Why, damn you!" Rader shouted in outrage. "I'll break your damned head for that."

He came off the wall like an enraged cat and rammed his shoulder under Newman's chin. There was momentum and outrage in the movement, and the force clicked Newman's teeth together. Newman was slammed against the edge of the bunk, and his knees buckled. He sat down suddenly, his bewilderment growing.

Rader stood over him, one hand on his shoulder, holding him down. "You wild man!" Rader shouted. "Listen to me. There's a gun leveled at you. Another try like that, and Andy will blow your head off." He glanced at Anderson. Anderson stood in the doorway of the cell. His face was strained but determined.

"If he tries anything else, Andy," Rader called, "shoot him."

Anderson tightened his grip on the gun and nodded.

Rader was satisfied. Anderson would do what he had to do.

"I ain't going to prison for five years!" Newman shouted.

He tried to rise, and Rader slammed him back onto the bunk. "That's already been decided," he said grimly. "I can't do anything about it. Hold out your hands."

Newman stared blankly at him.

"Damn it," Rader said furiously. "Do you want me to take off those cuffs, or do you want to sit in here with them on?"

The question got through to Newman, and his eyes cleared. He held out his hands.

Rader unlocked the cuffs. "You sit right here until I get outside. You hear me?"

Newman nodded. His mouth was a thin, strained line. "I ain't going to prison," he said. "You'll see."

Rader was angry to the point of violence, but he restrained himself. This hulk had given him more trouble than the last half-dozen prisoners.

"You want something to eat?"

"I ain't hungry," Newman said sullenly.

Rader shrugged. "Suit yourself." He thrust the cuffs into a hip pocket, and walked out of the cell. He slammed the door and locked it.

"I didn't like that, Quincy," Anderson said shakily.

Rader chuckled. "You showed it."

"Hell," Anderson said in self-defense. "I'm no gunman."

"Don't fret over it," Rader said calmly. "If anything was needed, you would have done it."

Anderson grinned wryly. "I'm glad it didn't come to that. How dangerous is he, Quincy?"

"Plenty," Rader said laconically. "He's a trapped animal, and the walls are closing in about him. It wouldn't take much more to break him completely. I know one thing. I won't go in that cell alone. He's desperate enough to jump me at any time." He grinned at the distress stealing across Anderson's face. "Quit sweating. I'm not asking you to hang around. Harl will be back shortly."

"That relieves me," Anderson confessed. "I wouldn't have your job, Quincy."

"You'd get used ot it," Rader replied.

As they approached his desk, he asked, "How would you like a belt to steady your nerves?"

"I'd like it," Anderson replied promptly. "My God! Will you look at that." He held out a hand and it was shaking.

Rader pulled a bottle out of the desk and found two glasses. He filled them and said, "I'm glad you didn't have to shoot. You could've hit me."

At his grin Anderson said crossly, "It's all too damned true. Do you expect more trouble from him, Quincy?"

Rader's face was serious. "His kind are the most dangerous. They're so damned near falling off the edge, a man never knows when it will happen. I'll be glad to see him step into that wagon."

"You won't try to load him alone?" Anderson asked.

"No siree," Rader said vehemently. "Harl will be around. If Newman does crumble, I've got a hunch it'll be when he sees the tumbleweed wagon. That's when he'll know he's too close to prison to escape." He sipped at his drink. "Andy, I've got a hunch the judge didn't sentence the right man. I still believe Temple was behind Hiram's death from the beginning."

"My feeling, exactly. I was positive Newman would break before the trial was over." He sighed and finished, "But he didn't."

Rader took a ragged breath. "Damned shame. What's going to happen to Harl now?"

"It's already happened. You served the eviction notice."

"I know that," Rader said impatiently. "Are you saying there's no out for Harl?"

Anderson slowly shook his head. "You saw how public opinion is against Temple. It might force him to hold a foreclosure sale. But that wouldn't do Harl any good. He won't be able to raise the money he needs." He shrugged. "Anything the sale brings above what Harl owes would have to be paid to him. But it won't happen."

"What makes you so damned positive?" Rader asked crossly. "The Bow Gun's worth more than the debt against it."

"Before the winter it was," Anderson said. "And it will be later. But now, who's got that kind of money?"

Rader considered that. "Nobody that I know of. I was hoping Harl would come out with a few dollars." His face was set as he refilled his glass. "It's a damned shame," he repeated. "You and I both know we're seeing a miscarriage of justice. And maybe Hambert suspects it."

"Yes," Anderson acknowledged. "And there's not a

damned thing we can do about it." He reached for the bottle again.

The afternoon passed with few words exchanged. Every now and then, one of them muttered an oath as they sipped at their whiskey.

Harl walked into the office just before dark. He looked at the bottle and the drinks and jeered, "Is this the way city officials spend their on-duty time?"

"Not usually," Rader replied solemnly. "But Andy and I figure we had this one coming. We had a little trouble earlier."

Harl's eyes widened. "From Newman," he breathed. He saw the bruise on Rader's cheek for the first time. "Did he hit you?"

"I went into his cell to take the cuffs off him," Rader said, chagrined. "He swung both hands at me. Knocked me into a wall. I know better than to get careless like that." He felt his cheek and swore. "Say! It is tender." He shook his head in wonder. "I gave Andy my gun to keep Newman covered while I went in. Damned good thing I did."

Harl waved aside the proffer of a drink. "Newman is dangerous," he commented. "Do you think Hambert was too severe?"

Rader shook his head. "I don't. Somebody deserved to pay. Newman was just a gullible tool, pushed by Temple. Temple wanted the Bow Gun."

Harl stared bleakly across the room. A man could start a day and never have the slightest idea twenty-four hours would change his life. It certainly had turned out that way for him. He could see no way to pin the blame on the man responsible.

Anderson tried to lift Harl's spirits. "Everybody who witnessed that trial feels the same way, Harl. Temple's the man we want, but he goes free."

Harl swore bitterly. "I talked to Charley Duncan for a

few minutes before I came in. Temple fired him for his testimony."

Rader banged his fist on the desk in an excess of rage. "So Ira gets everything he wanted, and we can't stop him." He shook his head and reached for the bottle.

All three of them were lost in sober reverie. Footsteps coming through the door broke their trance.

"Good afternoon, Mrs. Newman," Rader said almost apologetically.

Harl felt sorry for her. The strain lines in her face spoke eloquently of the hard time she was going through.

She wanted to ask something, but she was too timid to speak. She kept fumbling around, turning the shabby purse over and over in her hands.

"What can I do for you, Mrs. Newman?" Rader asked gently.

"Could I see my man?" she managed to get out. "I need to talk to him bad."

Distress clouded Rader's eyes. "I can't let you see him alone."

Tears threatened to spill out of her eyes. "Why not?" she asked plaintively. "I've got some things to say that only Mungo should hear."

Rader shook his head. "Sorry. I can't let you see him alone. I can't risk you slipping him a gun or a knife."

She angrily dabbed at her eyes. "Isn't my word enough?"

Rader looked pained as he continued to shake his head. "I'm afraid it isn't."

She held out her purse. "Go ahead. Search it. You'll find I'm not carrying anything in it."

Rader's face flamed. "Searching your purse wouldn't prove anything."

She caught what he meant, for she blushed. "You mean I'd have to be searched?"

Rader bobbed his head. "That's it, ma'am. I have no lady deputies. It'd be impossible."

Her face stiffened. "Go ahead and search me. It means that much for me to see Mungo."

Rader's breathing came harder. "I still can't let you see him alone." Distress spread over his face.

Harl couldn't stand to watch this any longer. "Quincy, how about if I went along?" At the objection forming in Mrs. Newman's face he said hastily, "You could talk in a low voice. I'd have to be close but not close enough to hear."

She struggled with her resentment, then finally said grudgingly, "If that's the way it has to be."

Rader still didn't like this new arrangement, but it had gone this far, and he didn't see a way to stop it.

"That's the way it has to be," he said firmly. His eyes were smoking as he glanced at Harl. "Harl, I'm holding you responsible if anything happens. You remember that."

Harl shrugged. "Sure."

Harl took Mrs. Newman's elbow and steered her to the aisle that ran alongside of the cells. Newman was in the next to the last one.

"Mungo," she cried and hurried the last few steps, her arms outspread.

Harl hastily caught up with her and blocked her passage with his body.

"You can't touch him, ma'am," he said stubbornly. "You heard the sheriff."

Her eyes clouded over. "What kind of a meeting is that?"

"The only one you can have. Stay three feet from the cell. If you try to touch him, I'll rush you right out of here. I'll move a few feet down the corridor. I won't listen."

Her face sagged with weary resignation. "If that's the only way."

Harl smiled. "Sorry, ma'am."

He moved away from her to a spot a couple of yards from Newman's cell. As long as she didn't try to touch Newman, Harl could see everything that went on.

Ruby glanced back at Harl and shook her head. Newman

immediately lowered his voice. "Don't cry, Ruby. I fixed it to take care of you. It's going to be all right. There's one thing I want you to do. See Mr. Temple. If he's not at the bank, go to his house. Do you know where it is?"

She nodded numbly. His frown stopped her from speaking. "I want you to tell him to get down here and see me. You put it hard. I don't want him to misunderstand. Can you do that, Ruby? It means everything to me."

"I guess I could," she whispered. "Oh, Mungo, I can't stand you being here."

"Neither of us can do anything about that now," he said. "Please, Ruby. Will you do as I ask? I'll be able to rest easier."

Tears leaked from her eyes. "If that's what you want," she said brokenly.

Harl was surprised when she rejoined him so soon. They had spent only a few minutes together.

Looking back, Harl saw Newman stumble to his bunk and sink down onto it, burying his head in his hands. He shook his head. Lord, the messes people got themselves into.

He glanced at Ruby Newman. She stared straight ahead, her eyes filled with tears, and her lips trembled. Odd little moaning sounds came from her mouth.

Rader looked questioningly at them as they stepped into the office. "That didn't take long," he said dourly.

Ruby broke into open sobbing. "Can I see him again?" she begged.

Rader wanted to refuse; it was written all over his face. He sighed and said, "I guess it'll be all right. But only for a moment or two."

Harl waited until Ruby left the office. "I don't know what they talked about. They whispered. I know you broke rules, but it did those two a lot of good."

"That's a charitable attitude for a man to have toward his father's murderer," Rader commented.

"I wasn't forgetting that," Harl said flatly. "But she didn't have anything to do with it."

Anderson shivered. "Just being here gives me the jitters. I'll be glad when he's gone."

Rader threw a half-smoked cigarette away. "Two of us," he said harshly. "Two of us."

Chapter Twenty

Temple's face was ashen as he thought of the talk last night with Newman's wife. No matter how much he protested that he didn't have time to see Newman, she had insisted. "Mungo says you'd better." Her fear showed in her face. "I don't know what he could do, Mr. Temple, but I think you'd better do as he says."

That was last night, and here it was almost evening. Temple had put off seeing Newman as long as he dared. His guts ached as he thought that Newman might talk to the authorities.

He walked along, his head bent low. Oh, Lord! Why were the authorities so lax in their duty? Newman was found guilty four days ago. Newman should have been taken from Miles City before now.

Only Rader was in the office when Temple stepped inside. "Could I see Newman?" Temple asked in a husky voice. "He did something for me while he worked at the bank. I've got to talk to him about it."

The sharpness in Rader's eyes cut clear through Temple. He thought Rader was going to refuse, and Rader surprised him by saying, "I guess it would be all right. Just a couple of minutes, though."

Temple hastily agreed. His face was pinched with anxiety as Rader moved toward him. "What are you doing?" he bleated.

"I've got to search you before I can let you talk to Newman."

"I wouldn't try to take a weapon to him," Temple said indignantly.

"I'll be the judge of that," Rader snapped. "I've seen some things I never believed would happen. Hold out your arms."

Temple submitted to the search. Rader's hands deftly went over him. He finished and said, "All right. I'll be at the end of the corridor, watching you. Don't try anything foolish, Ira."

"Do you think I'm crazy?" Temple demanded.

"Nothing would surprise me any more," Rader snapped.

He led Temple to Newman's cell and said, "You've got a couple of minutes. No more." Rader retreated to the end of the corridor.

Out of the corner of his eye, Temple could see Rader standing there.

Newman started to speak, and Temple whispered, "Keep your voice down, you fool. Do you want Rader hearing you?"

Newman seared him with a look but remained silent.

"Why did you send Ruby to see me?"

"You know damned well why," Newman said in a low, passionate voice. "You didn't pay her anything. You promised me you'd give Ruby twenty-five hundred dollars if I was sentenced." Bitterness filled his voice. "I got five years."

"Damn it," Temple said in an agonized bleat. "Keep your voice down. I was going to pay Ruby. But things came up—" His voice trailed off.

"I'll bet," Newman sneered. "Nothing you promised me came true. Now I want more money. I want Ruby to have five thousand dollars."

"That wasn't our agreement," Temple moaned.

"It is now, or I'll tell the authorities what really happened. You get that money to Ruby right now. She'll let me know when she gets it."

Temple's face looked as though he were suffering actual

physical pain. "That's a lot of money, Mungo. It'll take me some time to raise it."

"Today," Newman snapped. He turned and walked to the back of the cell.

Temple looked as though he had shrunk in size when he rejoined Rader.

"That didn't take long," Rader observed. He noticed the gray face and said, "You look sick, Ira. What passed between you two?"

"I wish to God I'd never hired him," Temple said in a broken voice. "I'll be glad when he's gone."

Rader felt no sympathy for Temple. "Maybe your concern about Newman is over. I got a wire early this morning that the tumbleweed wagon will pick him up in the morning."

Temple's shoulders straightened, and the distressed look left his face. Could he stall Newman until tomorrow? Once Newman was in the wagon, the immediate pressure would be relieved.

Rader watched Temple leave the office with a speculative gleam in his eyes. Something had happened back there. He'd give a lot to know what it was.

Rader was still frowning when Harl came in after a round of the town. "You look like you've bitten into something bad," Harl commented.

"I have," Rader grunted. "Temple was just here, talking to Newman."

Harl's eyes sharpened. "What did he want?"

Rader shook his head. "I can't tell you. I couldn't hear what passed between them. But one good thing happened. While you were out, Jones brought me a telegram. The tumbleweed wagon is coming in the morning."

"Well, that's some improvement," Harl said. "Don't look so concerned. I'm just a little down. With Newman gone, I guess we'll never get at the truth."

He took a restless turn about the office. "That's one job I

wouldn't want. Driving desperate men to prison." He shuddered as he thought of how wearing it must be on a driver's nerves.

"Wirt's been doing it for ten years," Rader said. "Guess he's gotten used to it."

"Rader," Newman yelled, "I want to talk to you!"

The volume of the yell startled Rader, for he jumped. "He expects instant service," he said sourly. His voice raised, "I'll be back there later. I'm busy."

"Now," Newman insisted. "It's important."

Rader sighed and climbed to his feet. "Both of us will be glad when he's gone." He walked toward the cells.

He came back a few minutes later, shaking his head.

"What's he want?" Harl asked.

"He demanded to see Ruby."

"Does he expect us to take him to her?"

Rader laughed shortly. "Not quite that bad. But he wants to get word to her to come down here."

"What'd you tell him?"

"I told him I'd try to work it in. Harl, on your next round, drop in and see Mrs. Newman. Tell her Mungo wants her."

He sat down, his face heavy. "Tomorrow can't come too soon for me."

Harl grinned and reached for his hat. "Might as well get it over." He strode toward the door.

Harl hadn't been gone ten minutes when Newman yelled again. "Did you get word to her, Rader? I tell you this is important."

He kept up the yelling until Rader couldn't stand it any longer. He walked back to the cells, his strides angry with purpose.

"You listen to me, Newman. I'm sick of your yelling your head off. I've sent word to your wife. You keep up this yelling, and I won't let you see her."

Newman's tone changed. "If you knew how important

this is, you'd be a little sympathetic. It could be important to you, too."

Rader swore in disgust and walked away from the cell.

Harl was gone for almost an hour. Rader blew out a relieved sigh when he returned. "He's been yelling his head off every ten minutes. Did you get in touch with her?"

Harl nodded. "She said she'd be here as fast as she can."

"I hope so," Rader grumbled.

She came in twenty minutes after Harl. She breathed hard, and she was literally shaking. "Is something wrong?" she pleaded.

"Nothing wrong," Rader answered. "Except your man is a big mouth. He won't give me any peace. Every few minutes, he yells that he has to see you."

Her face flooded with a rush of hope. "Then I can see him?"

"Under the same conditions as before. I'll give you a couple of minutes. No more. Is that understood?"

She nodded mutely, and Rader led her to Newman's cell. "Get your talking over," he said gruffly. "You haven't got long."

He backed to the end of the corridor and watched them with agate eyes.

Ruby started to say something, and Newman interrupted. "We haven't got time for that. Go to Temple. He's got some money for you. Take it and leave."

"How much money?" she whispered.

"Five thousand dollars." At her gasp, he said fiercely, "It's money I earned. Damn it, it's all for you. Don't argue with me. Just do as you're told. When you get the money, get back here and tell me."

"I don't know if the sheriff will let me see you again," she said timorously.

"He will," Newman said grimly, "or I'll raise so much hell he won't be able to take it."

"What if Mr. Temple refuses to give me the money, Mungo?"

Newman's face turned raw and violent. "He'd better, if he knows what's good for him. Now get."

Rader looked curiously at her as she approached him. Her face was so strained and pale. "Anything wrong?"

She shook her head. "Nothing wrong. It's just that it tears me apart every time I see him in here."

Rader nodded sympathetically. That wasn't hard to understand.

He joined Harl in the outer office. After Ruby left, he said, "She's going through hell."

Harl nodded. "I can imagine."

All during the afternoon, Newman kept yelling for Ruby. Each time Rader went back to shut him up, Newman asked if Ruby had returned.

"I told you I'd let you know if she shows up again."

Newman gripped the bars until his knuckles whitened. "I've got to see her one more time," he pleaded. "Then I won't bother you no more."

"Not much longer, anyway," Rader said harshly.

Newman's eyes went round and shining. "What do you mean by that?"

"The tumbleweed wagon comes tomorrow." If Rader had ever seen fear, he saw it now in Newman's face.

"Not tomorrow," Newman said in a choked voice. "There's something I've got to find out about."

"Tomorrow," Rader said firmly.

"Get word to Ruby I've got to see her," Newman begged. "Just one more time. That's all I'll ask for."

"I'll try to get word to her," Rader said wearily. Anything to shut Newman up.

Rader sent Harl twice during the afternoon to get word to Ruby. Each time, Harl returned, shaking his head. "Not home, Quincy."

"Jesus!" Rader exclaimed. "He'll howl now."

Newman kept up his yelling until Rader shut the inner door. That muted Newman's voice until it was bearable. "Now, he's asking for Temple. He demands that he talk to him again," Rader said in a worried voice. "Harl, by the way he's building up, I think he could go out of his head. That's one customer I'll be glad to hand over to Wirt."

Rader went back to the cells only once more, and that was to ask Newman if he wanted supper. Newman cursed him until Rader's cheeks reddened.

"You keep up that kind of talk, and I'll come in there and bust your head."

Rader stalked down the corridor and slammed the inner door again. "He refuses to eat. It doesn't bother me. It saves me from making a trip to the restaurant."

"He sure does a lot of yelling," Harl commented. "He wants something bad."

"He does," Rader growled. "He wants to see Ruby, then Temple. If he had his way, he'd be asking for half of the town. There's something back of that killing we haven't found out." He shrugged and rolled a cigarette. "All we can do is to wait and see if it comes out. The sorry part is there isn't much time left."

Chapter Twenty-one

It was getting dark when Rader lit the lamp. "You better go get something to eat, Harl."

"Not hungry yet. I'll get something later." Harl turned his head at a new yell from Newman. "He's at it again."

Rader ignored the outburst. "After you eat, you better turn in."

Harl shook his head. "I'm staying here with you."

Rader scowled at him. "Don't you think I can handle it?"

Harl grinned cheerfully. "Never doubted it. But with a wild man like that on your hands, even you could run into trouble."

Rader's leathery face relaxed. "Thanks, Harl," he said gruffly.

"Sure, Quincy."

They sat there the better part of two hours, only occasionally breaking the silence with a word or two.

Harl stood and stretched. "My belly's beginning to complain. I'm going out and get a bite to eat."

"Bring me back a sandwich, Harl."

"You've got it, Quincy."

Harl returned as quickly as he could. He handed Rader two wrapped sandwiches and grinned at the startled flash in Rader's eyes. "I know what you ordered," Harl said softly. "I found out I was hungrier than I thought. It could happen to you."

He sat down and watched Rader eat. The muted sound of Newman's yelling drifted to him. "He's still at it."

"Hasn't shut up," Rader said in disgust. "He's got good lungs, even if his head lacks a little."

He finished the second sandwich and grinned at Harl's sardonic glance. "You were right," he said cheerfully. "Now, if we could take care of the sleep as easily as the eating."

He put his boot heels up on his desk and tried to get comfortable.

Harl stirred restlessly. This was going to be a long and arduous night. He barely closed his eyes when Newman's yelling reached him again.

Rader's heels hit the floor with a bang. "Damn him," he said wrathfully. "I'm going back there and break his head."

"Easy, Quincy," Harl advised. "It's only a few hours until daylight."

"You're gonna find out how long those few hours are going to be."

Both men spent a miserable night, and both were awake with the first faint light of dawn.

Rader stomped about the office, trying to stretch his muscles. "Oh, Lord," he groaned. "I feel like I'm going to break in two."

"Me too," Harl said sourly. "I was hoping we wouldn't wake up so early. We've still got some hours before that wagon comes."

"Don't you think I know that," Rader said in a surly tone. "Will you go down to Ma Summer's. She opens about now. Bring Newman some breakfast. It might be a long time before he has another chance to eat. Better eat your own breakfast while you've got the chance."

"Can I bring you something, Quincy?"

"Not another sandwich," Rader replied sourly.

The better part of an hour passed before Harl could return. "Ma was just opening when I got there," he explained. "I had to wait until she got her fires started." He placed two trays before Rader. "Brought you a tray, too." He uncovered one of the trays. "How does scrambled eggs and a piece of ham sound to you? Better eat while it's still warm."

Rader drank his cup of coffee before he attacked his food. "I needed that." His voice brightened. "Appreciate this, Harl."

He was halfway through his breakfast when the yelling started again. "I don't believe it," Rader said. "I heard him yelling most of the night, and he's at it again."

He stood and picked up the second tray Harl brought. "Maybe this will shut him up."

"You'd better finish your breakfast," Harl advised. "It'll get cold."

"I'd rather eat it cold than listen to him yell. Coming with me?"

Newman was standing at the bars when he saw them coming. "You'd better get Ruby or Temple down here," he threatened.

"Or what?" Rader asked wearily.

"Or you'll be damned sorry."

"I'm damned sorry I ever laid eyes on you," Rader said hotly. "I brought you your breakfast."

"I don't want it. I want to talk to Ruby or Temple."

Rader turned his head toward Harl. "Keep him covered, Harl. I'm going to put his breakfast on his bunk. What he does with it after that I don't give a damn."

Rader unlocked the door, and under the coverage of Harl's gun walked past Newman and set the tray down.

He came back out and relocked the door. "Let's go, Harl."

Harl blew out a weak breath. "I was afraid he would try something."

Rader shook his head. "Not with your gun on him."

Harl looked over his shoulder. "Think he'll eat?"

"He will, if he's hungry enough. I'm not worrying about it." Rader sat down at his desk and resumed eating. "It's all Newman's picking. If he wants to travel on an empty stomach, it's all right with me." He looked out into the street and dolefully shook his head. "If I had one wish right now, do you know what it would be?"

Harl grinned. "You haven't told me yet."

"I wish I was big enough and powerful enough to get behind the sun and push it higher into the sky."

Harl whistled softly. "You really want to get rid of him, don't you?"

"I want that so bad I hurt," Rader said savagely.

Chapter Twenty-two

The hours dragged slowly by. Newman never stopped yelling.

"Determined, ain't he?" Harl asked wearily.

"He's plumb wore me out," Rader confessed. "It can't go on much longer."

Harl walked to the window and looked out. "Something's happening down there," he observed. "Crowd gathering."

Rader joined him and looked down into the street. "No wonder they're gathering," he said slowly. "The wagon's coming."

Harl had never seen a tumbleweed wagon before, but he knew this had to be it. The approaching wagon was a drab, deadly-looking vehicle. It was painted black and roofed over. Harl watched it pull up and stop before the jail. The only window he could see was barred. "Hell of a thing, Quincy," he said soberly.

"Yes," Rader answered in a tight voice.

A chunky man was just climbing down from the driver's seat. He stared at the sheriff's office, then reached into the wagon and pulled out leg irons and handcuffs. Harl had never looked at a harder-faced man.

"Tough-looking cuss, Quincy."

"He's as tough as he looks," Rader assured Harl. "If he's lost any prisoners, I never heard about it."

Harl nodded. Wirt looked completely capable. "He's been driving that wagon for ten years?"

"Something like that."

"It hasn't bothered him much," Harl observed.

"It's changed him in one way," Rader said. "He's hardened." Strain etched deep lines in Rader's face. "Oh, oh," he exclaimed. "Ruby just came up and joined the crowd."

"Oh hell," Harl muttered. It was going to be bad enough for Newman to climb into that wagon, but having his wife watch made it far worse.

"This damned day," Rader said, and it was a prayer for it to end.

Wirt came into the office, carrying a rifle, and there was a pistol in his holster. He was ready for any contingency.

"Hello, Rader," Wirt said, shifting the rifle from his right to his left hand.

Rader's reluctance to shake hands with Wirt showed, and Harl thought he understood the reason. Wirt had an air of cruelty about him. Harl guessed a man would have to develop that trait to be able to endure on this job.

Rader introduced Harl and said, "Harl Stark. He's replacing Grimson."

Wirt eyed Harl curiously. "He looks pretty young."

Harl stiffened. Wirt meant soft instead of youthful.

Rader stepped quickly to Harl's defense. "He does his job," he said curtly.

Wirt's grin showed that Rader's rebuke hadn't set him back any. "Stark," he mused. "Wasn't it the Stark murder trial that made some work for me?"

"The same," Rader replied. Out of deference for Harl's feelings, Rader didn't want to go into intimate details. "Are you ready to pick up your prisoner?" he snapped.

Wirt's grin didn't change. "That's what that wagon means, doesn't it?"

"This way." Rader headed for the cells. "He's a big one," he warned.

"That wagon cuts the biggest ones down to size," Wirt said, unperturbed.

"He can be hard to handle," Rader said, his lips thin. "He's been under a lot of strain."

"I've never had any complaints about not being able to handle my job," Wirt said sharply.

He stopped in front of Newman's cell, his head tilted as he appraised the prisoner. "He is big, isn't he?"

Newman guessed who Wirt was, for his face went taut. His eyes started that wild rolling again. "The wagon's here?" he asked in a thick, choked voice.

"It's here," Rader answered. He had no reason to like Newman, yet he couldn't help but feel pity for him.

"I ain't going," Newman screamed, "until I talk to Ruby or Temple."

"You come along easy, boy," Wirt said, "and nobody has any trouble. Of course, you can have it the other way. I try to please."

"Temple isn't coming," Newman cried, and there was sheer desperation in his voice.

"Don't look like it," Rader said softly.

"Wait," Newman pleaded. "I've got to talk to Judge Hambert. I can tell him something that will change everything."

"You waited too long," Rader said solemnly. "The judge left town two days ago."

"Come on, boy," Wirt said impatiently. "There's been too much talking already." He handed his rifle to Rader, the pistol to Harl. "Unlock the door. Keep him covered until I get him shackled."

Rader nodded and unlocked the door. Wirt entered the cell, and Newman retreated before him. Spittle flecked his lips. "Wait," he kept saying hoarsely. "I've got to—"

Wirt made an impatient slash of his hand. "The only thing you've got to do is stop this damned nonsense. You better stand still. I won't tell you again. I can put these irons on after I knock you out. It'll be a hell of a lot easier on you this way."

He kept up his inexorable advance until Newman was

backed into a corner. Newman stood there shivering, his hands held out in mute supplication.

This was old stuff to Wirt, and long experience had made his hands quick, his motions sure. He judged the distance to Newman's wrists, and the cuffs flashed in his hand. Harl heard the click as the cuffs closed.

"That wasn't so bad, was it, boy?" Wirt asked, pleased with himself.

"You two watch him close," Wirt ordered Rader and Harl. "Even after they're cuffed, I've had them try to kick my head off when I stooped to leg-iron 'em."

Newman read menace in Wirt's face, and his resistance completely faded. "Won't anybody listen to me?" he moaned.

Wirt finished snapping on the leg irons. He turned and headed Newman toward the door. "Your listening time's all gone, boy." He shoved Newman forward. "Get moving."

Newman shuffled down the corridor, the leg irons clanking.

Harl and Rader followed the pair ahead of them. Harl wondered if his face was as set and bleak as Rader's.

Rader checked Wirt before he stepped outdoors. "I need your signature," he snapped.

Wirt grinned. "Damn, I almost forgot that." His face worked as he bent over to scrawl his name on the form Rader placed before him.

Wirt pushed the form back at Rader, then prodded Newman with the rifle muzzle. "Time to go, boy."

The crowd had grown by the time they walked outside. Wirt hummed a tune as he glanced about at the crowd.

Harl looked at Ruby. Her face was pitifully white, and her lips were drawn back in a ghastly grimace. "Mungo," she screamed.

Newman was at the foot of the two steps to the door in the back of the wagon. Wirt was right behind him, alert for any move Newman might try to make.

Ruby's scream reached Newman, and he stopped and turned.

"Mungo," she called. "I tried to see him. He wasn't at the bank, and he wouldn't open his house door to me."

Newman's face turned frantic. "You've got to see him. If he doesn't pay, tell him—"

Wirt prodded him with the rifle. "Climb those steps, boy." The jab of the rifle muzzle had to be painful.

Newman turned and climbed to the top step. He paused again.

"Mungo!" Ruby cried. It was a long, drawn-out wail, sounding like a mortally wounded animal.

Newman started to turn. "Ruby!" he shouted. "I'll be back. I promise you—"

Wirt struck out viciously with the rifle barrel. He hit Newman across the forehead. Newman stiffened, his face going shocked and slack. A curtain of blood dropped across Newman's face before he fell.

Wirt was a quick and efficient worker. He grabbed Newman by the legs and shoved him into the wagon. He slammed the door shut and locked it.

"That shows how wrong he was," he announced and showed yellow teeth.

"Damn it," Rader exploded. "That man is hurt. Are you going to give him attention before you start out?"

"Them kind always have hard heads," Wirt said, his grin reappearing, "or they wouldn't be in this spot. He'll come out of it. Best way to start out is to show them who's boss. I've got a long way to go. He'll be easier to handle."

Rader was breathing hard. A calculating look shone in his eyes as he remembered that crazed look that could seize Newman's face.

Wirt correctly read that look. "I'm the one who's got to worry about him," he said flatly.

Ruby was struggling in the arms of two bystanders, trying to fight her way to the wagon.

"Keep her back," Rader called.

He waited until Wirt climbed up onto the driver's seat. He didn't return the man's wave. The wagon started rolling slowly down the street.

Rader shook his head at the distress in Harl's face. "A rotten job for anybody involved in this kind of human misery," he growled.

"There's not much anybody can do for her right now," Harl said, breathing hard.

Rader nodded. "You're so damned right, Harl."

Chapter Twenty-three

Newman's head ached intolerably. He tried to recall where he was, but the pain was so intense that he couldn't concentrate. He seemed to be floating on one vast sea of agony, and the sea was a vicious force, hitting him with constant jolts and jars. But worst of all was that he couldn't see. No matter how hard he tried, he couldn't penetrate the thick, black veil before his eyes.

His cuffed hands handicapped him, but by twisting and partially rolling, he could scrub at that black veil with his fingers. Digging at the curtain wasn't painful, and he doggedly kept at it. He wanted to yell his relief when a thin glimmer of light penetrated the curtain. He wasn't blind; he had dug rents in that veil.

He dug harder, and the rents broadened. He felt something sticky on his hands, and the memory of what had happened to him came back. The driver of the wagon had knocked him unconscious.

Now Newman understood that floating sensation. He was in the wagon. Every now and then a bump jolted the wheels. He was on his way to prison, and terror welled over him.

He wanted to scream against the terror, and he picked at the caked blood that still impaired his vision. That helped occupy his mind, still it was all he could do to keep from breaking into a sob.

God, he was so thirsty. It was early in the season and not inordinately hot for this time of the year. But the close confines of the wagon made it seem unbearably hot. Maybe if he could make the driver hear him, he would stop and give him a drink.

Newman yelled until his lungs ached, then gave up. Either the driver didn't hear him or chose to ignore him. He writhed on the floor. How long would this torment go on; when would his head quit aching.

It was still daylight. Newman could tell by the late sunshine streaming in through the right window of the wagon. If only the pounding in his head would subside, maybe he could think rationally. This wagon had to stop sometime. Maybe he would have to wait until nightfall to be heard, but the wagon would stop.

He dozed off into a heavy, fitful slumber. Every now and then, a particularly bad bump jolted him into wakefulness. He lay there, sensing the motion. The wagon was still rolling.

Newman came out of that heavy stupor that was more like unconsciousness than sleep. He could no longer sense the wagon's motion, and no daylight streamed in through either window. It must be dark, or very close to it. The wagon had stopped.

Newman strained to hear movement outside the wagon. He thought he heard sounds of the horses being unhitched, and he screamed at the top of his lung power. He yelled until his voice became husky and faint. Nobody was going to hear him, or if they did, they didn't intend to give him any attention.

The door opened so suddenly that Newman blinked in surprise. He saw the dark silhouette of a man standing there and said petulantly, "You took your time. I yelled my head off for you."

"I heard you," Wirt replied. "I had to take care of the horses, then set up the night's camp." He was in a bad mood, for he lashed out, "Get it through your thick skull you're in no position to give orders of any kind. You take what's handed you. Do you understand that?"

"You hurt my head," Newman complained. "It hurts so bad I can hardly think."

"You're tearing me apart," Wirt said sardonically. "Come on. Get out of there."

Newman managed to get his feet under him. He almost stumbled going down the steps at the rear of the wagon. Wirt offered no assistance of any kind. He stood off to one side, rifle ready for any unwise move Newman might make.

Newman's hatred of this man rose in steady waves. God, if he could only get his hands on this unfeeling brute.

"Get over to that little tree," Wirt ordered. "Sit down by it."

Newman did as he was told. He was too drained to think of anything else, but the hatred kept pumping up within him. Somewhere along this misery route, he would find his chance.

Wirt leaned his rifle against another tree and pulled his pistol. He held it in his left hand and said, "One wrong move, and I'll blow your head off. All I've got to do is to deliver a body. Dead or alive. It don't make any difference to me."

He bent at Newman's feet and unlocked the leg irons, breathing hard as he straightened.

"Put your legs around that tree," Wirt ordered. "Just try any funny ideas, and you'll be dead before you know it."

Newman's legs were stiff and cramped. He thought briefly of trying to kick Wirt in the face, then decided against it. He was too beat up, and unwise haste might ruin all his chances. No, a better opportunity would come.

He put his legs around the tree, and Wirt relocked the leg irons.

"My head hurts," Newman mumbled. "Can I have some water?"

Wirt narrowly studied him. Maybe he had hit this man too hard. He didn't look right, and he sure didn't sound right. "That's reasonable enough," he said. "You keep your requests reasonable, and we'll get along."

He walked to his camp site, picked up a canteen, and returned. "Can you handle it?" he asked. "I brought along a rag, if you want to clean your face."

Newman reached eagerly for the canteen. Those damned cuffs made every movement awkward, but if a man was desperate enough, he could manage.

He got the cap off, raised the canteen to his lips, and drank in long, shuddering gulps. The water was tepid and brackish, but Newman had never tasted anything so good. His thirst slaked, Newman set about the difficult task of getting the cloth moistened. He dabbed at his face with the rag, and the last of the stickiness around his eyes disappeared.

By the light of the campfire he could see the pinkish stains on the cloth. He must have bled pretty good. No wonder he thought he had been blinded.

He sat there with narrowed eyes, watching Wirt move about the campfire, preparing supper. He was no longer an animal, driven by terror and reacting only on instinct. He was a thinking man, and somewhere along this tortuous journey his opportunity would come. Newman found then how deeply he could hate. He had never known anything like this before.

Wirt finally came over to him with a plate of beans and a cup of coffee. "Can you manage this?" he asked gruffly.

"I don't want anything to eat," Newman mumbled. "My head feels like it's falling off."

Wirt unfeelingly shook his head. "Better get used to this," he advised. "We've got four more days of travel." He set the beans and coffee down beside Newman. He shrugged and said, "Suit yourself about eating."

Newman drank most of the coffee. He didn't touch the beans. He could feed on his hatred.

He was awake most of the night. The campfire died to a

few embers, and Wirt's snoring drifted faintly to him. Newman wasted no effort, trying to get free of the tree between his legs. The leg irons stopped any effort. A conviction grew within him. He had to make a break and soon. He couldn't spend four more days traveling in that wagon.

He was awake with the dawn's first light. He saw Wirt move about, building his fire. Wirt opened a couple of cans and dumped out their contents into a pan. The pleasant aroma of boiling coffee drifted across the small clearing to Newman.

He lay sprawled on his back. He had spent the night in that uncomfortable position. He had to do the best acting of his life, he had to convince Wirt that the blow on the head had been too much, and he had slipped away into deep unconsciousness.

He shut his eyes as Wirt approached him. From now on, he would depend on his ears.

He sensed Wirt's presence right beside him. Wirt prodded him with a boot toe. "Hey, wake up. You ready for breakfast?"

He kicked Newman a little harder. "Ain't no use trying to fool me. Smarter ones have tried that."

Wirt mumbled to himself as he received no response. "Say!" he exclaimed. "He didn't eat any supper, either. Did I hit him too hard?" He made a round of Newman's body, muttering, "Possible, possible." He prodded Newman in the ribs with several jabs of the rifle muzzle.

Newman had two enemies that could betray him; his rage and the pain. He kept his eyes closed, his breathing slow and sallow.

"Damn it," Wirt complained. "I didn't hit him that hard. He must have banged his head in the wagon." He swore softly and bitterly. "It's going to be a chore to get this hulk loaded." Wirt kicked Newman again before he returned to his breakfast.

Through the tiny slits of his eyelids, Newman watched

Wirt eat. This position was getting more painful, and he wanted to move, but he couldn't risk his one big chance by seeking relief for his cramped muscles. Wirt's alert eyes would notice any change in his position. Wirt was coming his way again, and Newman closed his eyes. He felt Wirt's presence right beside him.

"Hey you!" Wirt yelled. He swore when Newman didn't move. He drove his boot toe into Newman's ribs. Newman's tightly clamped lips cut off a groan. God knew he felt like groaning. He had one solid idea in his mind. He could stand any pain until Wirt was finally convinced he was unconscious.

"You're not fooling me any," Wirt said, but the uncertainty was plain in his tone. He had one hell of a chore on his hands now. He had to drag this big hulk to the wagon, then hoist him inside.

Wirt was suddenly furious with this insensible man, and he wanted to kick him to pieces. But that would only make it that much more difficult to get him into the wagon, and if he didn't deliver, he didn't get paid. Worse, he could lose his job.

Wirt had to get Newman free of the tree, and he held his pistol in his left hand as he bent over the leg irons. "Just try something," he promised in a rage-thickened voice. "And I'll blow you to pieces."

He got the leg irons unlocked without any trouble, and his senses sharpened. If Newman was going to attempt a break, it would come now.

He kicked Newman again. By God, this hulk had to be unconscious. No man could take those kicks without reacting. Wirt hadn't seen a single twitch, not even a wince of pain across Newman's face.

"He's out," he muttered. He thought callously about Newman dying sometime during the night.

Wirt put the pistol back into its holster, grabbed Newman

by the shoulders, and started dragging him toward the wagon.

He stopped and mopped his perspiring face. Damn but Newman was a lot of weight to haul clear over to the wagon.

He looked hopefully at Newman, praying to see consciousness returning to his face. That dragging over the ground should have aroused a corpse.

He grinned cynically. Maybe that was what he had on his hands. It would be a lot easier to transport a dead man than to guard a live one.

Wirt dragged Newman to the foot of the steps. He thought he saw a small fluttering of the lips and bent his head nearer. He couldn't hear anything at the distance between them. He bent his head closer to make a more thorough check. If Newman was breathing, even faintly, he should feel it on his ear.

Wirt's head was only a couple of inches from Newman's face when the head on the ground rose with a ferocious force. Newman's head smashed Wirt full in the face, and Wirt felt his nose flatten. A blood-choked yell rattled around in his throat, and he grabbed frantically for his pistol. The blow to his head left his movement awkward and uncoordinated. Just as his hand closed on the gun butt, the head smashed him in the face again.

The force of the blow lifted Wirt almost upright, and he fell backward. That was another shocking blow, and his eyes swam. His vision was impaired, and his head was one huge drum of pain. He bled at the nose and mouth, and his thoughts threatened to slip away from him.

He still grabbed for his gun, and his dismay was one prolonged bleat of shock and horror. He must have drawn the gun far enough so that it cleared the holster, and the second blow had jarred it from his hand.

Fear was a hand seizing him by the throat, and its grip

was deadly. For the first time, he realized he was up against a madman, and without his weapons, he felt naked.

Newman flung himself on Wirt, crushing him back to the ground. His hands were awkward because of the handcuffs, but the fingers found Wirt's throat.

Wirt's hands flailed away at Newman's head and face. If he inflicted pain, he saw no indication. The guttural sounds coming from Newman's mouth were like those of an enraged animal.

The seeking thumbs found the base of Wirt's throat, and the balls of the thumbs located the socket at the base of the throat and dug in. The pressure was relentless, and Wirt's eyes started bulging. His face was turning black, and his hands flailed away in renewed desperation. His blows rattled off Newman's head and face, but the blows were becoming weaker. He flung his body from one side to the other. It made no difference which way he turned; he couldn't dislodge the tenacious burr clinging to him.

Newman squeezed Wirt's throat until his hands ached. Wirt's struggles were getting noticeably weaker. The former blows had lessened to a listless scraping of fingers across Newman's face. A shudder ran through Wirt's body, a long sigh escaped his mouth, and the mouth remained open, the lips slack.

Even after the body was limp, Newman didn't release the pressure on Wirt's throat. Only when he finally realized there was no resistance left in Wirt, did he lift his hands.

God, his lungs were on fire, and ragged gulps of air didn't seem to help. He rolled off Wirt's body and lay sprawled on the ground, his chest heaving. His face stung, and he lifted his hands to the painful scratches. He looked at his finger tips, and they were stained. He thought curiously about that for a moment, then nodded slowly. Wirt's fingernails had caused those scraped places.

He had to get these handcuffs off. There should be a key on Wirt's body. He found it awkward, trying to search

Wirt's pockets with his hands cuffed together. He caught the edge of one of the pockets and jerked savagely at it. The material split, and the contents of the pocket fell onto the ground.

Newman shook his head in frustration. All he could see were a few coins. He ripped off another pocket and found the ring of keys.

He was muttering and swearing by the time he got the proper key inserted into the lock of the handcuffs. He turned the key, and the cuffs fell away.

Newman stood, rubbing his chaffed wrists. He was weak and lightheaded, but otherwise he was fine. His belly rumbled, reminding him of how long it had been since he had eaten.

He found some cans of food under the seat of the wagon and built a hasty fire. A further search of Wirt's pockets produced some matches.

He got his fire going and watched the strengthening flames. Now he had to have something with which to open those cans, and he went back to Wirt's body. He picked a sheath knife out of its scabbard, and on second thought, removed Wirt's gun belt and holster. He picked up the pistol and dusted it off before he dropped it into the holster. There was no telling when he might need a gun.

He sawed the cans open with the heavy knife and dumped the contents into a pan, mixing beans, corn, and tomatoes into one unappetizing mess.

Newman placed the pan over the fire, but his ravenous hunger wouldn't let him wait until the food was thoroughly heated. He wolfed down the lukewarm food and flung the pan from him.

Newman stood and belched, his eyes summing up the possibilities the camp afforded. He would need one of the horses, and the fact he would have to ride bareback didn't bother him in the least.

He walked over to Wirt's body and picked up the rifle

lying nearby. He might need that. He kept the sheath knife, replacing it in its scabbard. There was no need to bury the body; the scavengers would dispose of it.

Newman was suddenly bone-wracking weary, but he couldn't stay here. Somebody passing could spot the wagon and investigate. No, he would have to move it deeper into the woods. After that was done he could travel after dark and keep off the road, and be relatively safe. He was going back to Miles City, to see Temple. That lying bastard had caused him all this misery. All he wanted was a chance to cram those lies down Temple's throat. That's where the knife would come in handy. It was silent and quick.

Newman unpegged the horse and clambered aboard. It wasn't much of a riding horse, but it was in good physical shape. It would take him back to Miles City with no difficulty.

Newman kicked his heels into the horse's flanks. The horse was reluctant to move under this new rider, and Newman had to kick it repeatedly to get it started.

He left the camp site without looking back. He had come out of this better than he hoped for. It was only proof that if a man was determined enough, he could accomplish whatever he set his mind to.

Chapter Twenty-four

It was odd how things stuck in a man's mind. Harl couldn't forget the scene where Newman was loaded into the wagon. That was bad enough, but it was Ruby's wail as she witnessed the same scene that made it unforgettable.

"You look troubled," Rader observed.

"Just thinking of Newman."

Rader grimaced. "I know. I thought about him all last night."

At least, Harl wasn't alone. "Wirt left day before yesterday, didn't he?"

Rader nodded. "About ten in the morning."

"Wonder how far he's gone," Harl mused.

"Not too far," Rader answered. "Fifty, maybe sixty miles. That wagon wasn't built for speed. Wirt won't hurry. I think he likes to see people suffer."

Harl shook his head. "It'll be a rough trip for Newman."

"For God's sake," Rader snapped. "Can't we quit talking about Newman and that damned wagon?"

"Sure," Harl said mildly. He stole covert glances at Rader. Maybe Rader was trying to cover up his real feelings.

The thud of running feet jerked both heads around. Al Jones, the telegraph agent, burst into the room.

"Quincy," he gasped. "This just came in—" He stopped to catch a breath. "Ran all the way," he wheezed. "Wait until you see this." He waved a telegraph form in one hand.

Rader eyed him curiously. "Take all the time you want, Al."

Jones's breathing eased, and he said in a more controlled voice, "I just copied this, Quincy. You won't believe it."

Rader had shown enough patience, and he yelled, "Will you get on with it?"

Jones looked solemnly from Rader to Harl. He was milking this moment for all the attention he could get. "You won't believe it," he repeated.

Rader banged the desk with his fist. "Goddamn it, Al. I'm not going to tell you again."

Jones cleared his throat. "Newman broke out of the tumbleweed wagon."

Rader's eyes widened. That was incredible. How could a shackled man break through a locked door? Wirt was an experienced man at his work, and his attention would never waver.

Rader jumped to his feet and grabbed the wire from Jones's hand. "Let me read that!"

He read silently at first, his mouth tightening with each word.

Harl fidgeted with impatience.

Rader raised his eyes and looked at Harl. "Wirt was found dead. The wagon was moved deeper into the woods. It doesn't give the time." He read from the wire again. "Wirt was throttled to death. It says he was horribly battered."

"Nothing about Newman?" Harl asked, his face intent.

Rader shook his head. "That's what the wire is for, to alert us he's on the loose. The sender suggests Newman could be heading this way."

He folded the telegram into a long, thin strip and beat it impatiently against his left hand.

"Quincy, don't tear that up," Jones cried. "I need it for my files. That's the only copy."

"Sure," Rader said absently and handed the folded slip of paper to Jones.

Jones straightened out the piece of paper, his face indignant.

Rader's eyes were far away, and Harl knew Rader was thinking ahead: which direction Newman would go.

"Quincy, do you think he'll try to get back here?"

"Who knows?" Rader said curtly. "Al, I don't want any talk of this getting around town. Right now, there's only three of us who know. If I hear any speculation, I'll know where it started."

Jones's face fell. "I won't say anything, Quincy."

Rader nodded. "Just be sure to keep it that way."

He waited until Jones left before he spoke. "That was a jolt, wasn't it?"

"It sure was, Quincy. How did Newman ever get free?"

Rader shook his head. "I never thought he could beat Wirt. But he did, and that's the important thing."

"Do you think he'll come back here?"

"Bound to, Harl. He's got two reasons. Ruby and Temple. I don't know which feeling is the stronger, but one or the other will draw him."

"Any idea when he could get here?"

"Only a pure guess. But I'd say it'll be after nightfall. I doubt he'll do any traveling until night. He's too well known around here."

Harl was lost in deep thought. "Which one do you pick? Ruby or Temple?"

"I'm picking Ruby," Rader answered. "He set a heap of store in that woman. He may go after Temple after he sees her, but I'm guessing he'll go to Ruby first."

"Will you tell Temple or Ruby about this, Quincy?"

"I have to," Rader replied heavily. "Temple's got a right to try and protect himself. I'm hoping Ruby can talk Newman out of whatever he has in mind." He sighed and stood. "Newman really dug himself a hole this time and pulled it in over him. This time, he won't get off with a sentence. He'll hang."

Harl thought of Ruby's despairing wail, and a shiver ran through him. Again, a woman would take the worst of the beating.

"What do you want me to do, Quincy?" he asked quietly.

"You go warn Temple that Newman's on the loose. I'll try to prepare Ruby. After that, you'd better stand by and watch Temple's house. I'll watch at Ruby's."

Harl hitched up his gun belt. "Could be a long night ahead, Quincy."

"A hell of a long one. The sad part is we don't know if it'll be tonight or tomorrow night. But you can bet he'll appear. Watch yourself, Harl. He's a damned desperate man now. Don't take a chance with him."

Harl swallowed hard. Rader made sense. Harl would treat Newman like a grizzly that had run amuck. There was no reasoning with such a creature. The only thing that would stop Newman was a bullet.

Chapter Twenty-five

It wasn't quite noon when Harl stopped by the bank, hoping to find Temple. A new man was in Duncan's cage, and he shook his head at Harl's inquiries. Harl had a slight acquaintance with Bentley.

"He's not in, Harl. He went out about fifteen minutes ago." He anticipated Harl's next question and said, "I don't know where he went. Maybe he's gone to lunch. He's about town someplace. Something big up?"

"What makes you ask that?" Harl asked evasively.

"The scowl on your face. You look like you bit into something sour."

"I've just got something on my mind," Harl said curtly.

Bentley shook his head, unconvinced. "I've got a hunch I won't last here long. I didn't much like taking Charley's place, but Temple offered me a good salary." He shrugged and grimaced. "You know the way things are."

"I sure do," Harl said with feeling. "I'm going to try and hunt up Temple." He looked back from the door.

Bentley was watching him curiously. Something was going on that Bentley couldn't fathom.

Harl hunted all over town for Temple. By inquiries, he learned that he had several times just missed him, and his irritation increased. How was he going to tell Temple that Newman was on the loose, if he couldn't catch up with him?

Harl made a last stop in the bank at four o'clock.

"Ira hasn't returned," Bentley said. "Maybe he went home early. You tried there yet?"

"No," Harl answered wearily. All during the afternoon,

the thought had strengthened that Temple's home was the logical place to find him. But Harl had stubbornly resisted the thought. He could easily run into Melody there, and he didn't want to see her.

He sighed and turned toward the Temple house. It was a big, white clapboard affair with a mansard roof. Pike had it built several years ago. It was a solid reminder of Pike's success.

Harl walked up to the door, raised hesitant knuckles, then knocked. The sound wasn't very loud, and it didn't carry much of a demand.

He groaned inwardly as he heard the light tap of feet approaching the door. That would be Melody. She always moved with such light grace.

Melody opened the door and frowned as she saw Harl. "Yes?" she asked in a chilling voice.

The rift between them was so wide that they could scarcely shout over it.

"Is Ira home?" he asked, and his voice was as cold as hers.

"Not yet," she replied, "but I expect him at any moment." She hesitated, showing her reluctance to offer the slightest hospitality. Finally she managed to say, "Won't you come in? You could wait for him here?"

Was that a tiny crack in her frozen facade. Harl grabbed at the opportunity. "I'd like that," he said gruffly. "It'd save me from making another trip."

· She was filled with curiosity as to his purpose, but she wouldn't ask. "Could I make some coffee, Harl? It won't take a moment."

He hadn't eaten since breakfast, and his belly was empty. "I'd like that," he said heartily. He followed her into the kitchen and sat on a stool, watching her bustle about. He was heartsore, and just watching her increased his torment.

Every now and then she glanced at him, then jerked her eyes away, color stealing into her cheeks. She wanted to say something to break this impasse, but he guessed a woman's stubbornness was as strong as a man's.

She opened the oven door, and a savory aroma drifted to Harl. He was hungrier than he realized.

"Say! That smells good," he burst out.

She flashed him a fleeting smile of appreciation. "I'm fixing a roast for supper. Would you like to try it?"

The juices were flowing in Harl's mouth, making his tongue thick and clumsy. He remembered other times he had spent here under happier circumstances. Then there was no chasm between them.

"I'd sure like that, Melody," he said huskily.

Melody cut a slab of beef and placed it between two thick slices of freshly baked bread. She poured a cup of coffee and handed it and the sandwich to him. "Be careful," she warned. "The beef is still hot."

He took a cautious bite of the sandwich. It wasn't too hot to be eaten.

Melody anxiously watched his sober face. "Is it all right?"

"It's wonderful," he said heartily.

The radiance started in her eyes and spread all over her face. It was almost like old times, Harl thought. It could be, flashed through his mind, if it wasn't for Ira.

He was just finishing the sandwich when they heard the front door open.

"That's Ira," Melody said in a precautionary tone.

Harl's face was a stolid mask when Temple came into the kitchen.

"You," Temple said disdainfully.

"I want to talk to you," Harl said calmly. Temple looked awful. Something was eating on him. His face was haggard, and his lips trembled.

"We've got nothing to talk about," Temple muttered. "It's all done. Nothing you can say will change things."

Harl's face clouded. It was hard to keep his dislike for this man from showing. "Your life could depend on what I have to say. You'd better listen."

"Nothing will change," Temple said. He saw the flash of temper in Harl's eyes and said sullenly, "Go ahead." He wouldn't look at Harl.

Harl didn't want Melody to hear this. The news could cause her unnecessary distress.

"We'd better talk in private," Harl suggested. Before he left the kitchen, he saw the coldness form in Melody's face again. That warm moment of a few minutes ago was gone.

Temple led the way into the parlor. He closed the door, then came back and said truculently, "I don't see where this is going to do you any good."

How Harl wanted to swear at him. He should walk away from this stubborn man and let him meet Newman by himself.

"Will you shut up and listen? We just got word this morning that Newman broke out of the tumbleweed wagon."

Temple's eyes bulged. He looked as though he would go into shock. He kept licking his lips, and when he finally could get the words out, they were labored and strained. "How could he get away? Wasn't there a guard with him?"

Harl nodded. "A tough one, named Wirt. Newman strangled him."

Temple's face turned ashen, and he looked as though he would break into tears. "Oh, my God," he moaned. "Does that mean he's on his way here?"

"Probably. You broke your promise to him. You made no attempt to see him. That's sticking in his mind." Harl's temper broke at the groveling man before him. "Think about it. He killed that guard to get back here."

"What am I going to do?" Temple whispered.

Sheer terror had given Harl control over Temple. "Protect yourself the best way you can. I'd advise not leaving this house. Not until we find Newman."

"Anything you say," Temple babbled.

"I'll keep an eye on the house tonight."

Gratitude started pouring out of Temple, and Harl flared. "I don't want your goddamned thanks." He touched the badge on his coat. "This says it's my job. Don't tell Melody anything about what we've discussed. It would only terrify her."

Temple nodded mute acquiescence.

Harl looked back from the door. This news had shattered Temple into a crumbled wreck. Harl wondered if he would ever recover. Probably not until Newman is caught, Harl thought. He closed the door gently behind him.

Chapter Twenty-six

It was early in the year, and night came quickly. Harl buttoned his sheepskin as the night wind strengthened. He had been completely around Temple's house, and he knew the grounds thoroughly. A light had come on in a room in the southwest corner, and Harl imagined that Temple occupied it. This was a two-story house, and soon after the first light appeared, another showed in an upstairs room.

Melody's room, Harl thought, looking at the lighted window. He was relieved she didn't know he was out here.

That sandwich wasn't going to hold him long. Sometime during the night, he would have to go someplace for a quick bite. No matter how short the meal, his absence would leave the house unprotected. Why should he be so concerned about that, he mused. It was ironic that he would even try to stop Newman from reaching Temple. He should turn and walk away and leave all this behind him. But he knew he wouldn't do that. Quincy was paying him to do a job, and Harl was grateful. He couldn't slap Quincy in the face by quitting.

He turned south, walking beside the house. It was warmer here, for the wind was cut off. When he reached the corner to head back north, he would be feeling the wind again. Its cutting power reminded him too much of winter and everything that had happened since then. Hiram had called the winter and its happenings an echo: an echo that came from every action, nature's and man's. Harl had learned one bitter lesson. There were a hell of a lot more bad echoes than good.

He ducked his head to avoid the blast of cutting wind. It made up his mind. Walking around the house as he was doing was ridiculous. If Newman did return, seeing Harl here would be a clear beacon that this was dangerous ground. Harl debated upon where he could take up a position. He couldn't find one spot from which to survey the entire house. He had to pick his spot by guesswork. He thought it likely that Newman would slink down the alley that ran behind the house, avoiding the well-traveled streets.

Harl decided the alley would be the most advantageous. That would be on the south side of the house and better sheltered. He took up his position beside a huge, old lilac bush. There was no use flogging himself with doubts as to the accuracy of his guesswork. Only the passing of time would point out whether or not he was right.

Time never passed quickly in inactivity. Harl wondered what the hour was. A glance toward the business district told him it wasn't late. Most of the town's lights were on. If Newman did come, it would probably be after midnight.

Glancing upward, he saw the light in the upper room go out. Melody had gone to bed. The light in the lower room burned on. Harl would bet that Temple wouldn't dare go to sleep tonight.

He chuckled mirthlessly as he pictured Temple's agonized pacing. The man would be plumb worn out before morning came.

The dull rumble of discontent in his belly kept reminding him he was hungry. Thinking about it only made it worse, for now the rumble was a raging sound, as though his belly were being squeezed by a giant hand.

Harl knew it was only going to get worse. The nearest restaurant was two blocks away, but he could make it there and back in a short time. He had instructed Temple to be sure all the doors were bolted. If Temple had followed that advice, Harl should get to the restaurant and back before Newman could begin to break in.

Harl nodded in sudden decision. He would race to the restaurant, order a couple of sandwiches of anything that was already cooked and hurry back. His decision made him feel guilty. At the moment, he had two masters, a sense of guilt and hunger. The hunger won.

Chapter Twenty-seven

Newman dismounted on the outskirts of town. He slapped the horse on the rump, dismissing it. He would not need it again. All he could think about was seeing Temple. What he would do after that, he hadn't decided.

It had been a long, tedious trip reaching town. He had kept off the roads, riding furtively through the timber. He doubted that anyone had seen him. Had Wirt's body been discovered? He shrugged with indifference. It didn't matter. But the possibility that Wirt's body had been found posed danger to him. Miles City could have been informed of Wirt's death and of his escape. That didn't matter, either. All he wanted was to reach Temple.

He would keep to the back streets and alleys, passing through them like a drifting shadow. No one would see him either, on this stage of his journey. He looked at the rifle he was carrying, then tossed it away. He wouldn't need it. He had the pistol and the knife.

Newman was strung tight, and he was hungry. He should have taken more food from Wirt's camp site, but the desire to get his hands on Temple overrode all other considerations.

He started working his way toward Temple's house. He knew it well from the outside, but he had never been inside. The first house he passed was a small, frame house, lonely in its isolation. No human eye saw him, but a dog barked furiously until Newman was long past the house. Dogs could be his real danger. They had keener sight and an acute sense of smell. If a dog's barking was prolonged enough, it would arouse human curiosity to seek the cause.

There was no fear in Newman's thinking. Only the solid core of his determination remained. He had suffered to come this far; he couldn't be stopped now.

Stealthily, he worked his way ever closer to Temple's house. Temple had lied to him; he had ignored his promise to give him the money for Ruby. Even now, she could be suffering. Newman growled deep in his throat.

His muscles ached with fatigue, and it took great effort to force himself on. But the flame of hatred, burning fiercely in his mind supplied energy his muscles could not give.

Would he try to see Ruby after he finished with Temple? He let the question slip from his mind. It was too big to think about now.

Fatigue temporarily left him as he came in sight of the white house. His throat was tight with rage as he saw the light burning in the downstairs room. Somebody was awake. He prayed it would be Temple.

Newman made a cautious round of the house, his eyes questing to spot every shadow, trying to learn if it held a threat for him. He saw nothing alarming. If the news of his escape had reached Miles City, Temple hadn't heard about it, or had done nothing to protect himself.

Animal instinct told him not to try and force the doors. They would be locked, and the noise of his breaking in would warn the occupants of the house. It could also carry to somebody outside. He hoped to find an unlocked window. He could slip in through it, then work his way to the lighted room.

He went cautiously along the house, testing every window. Disappointment was beginning to flow through him. He wasn't sure just what he would do, if he found all the windows secured. He supposed he would have to break the glass, which posed the danger that the breaking glass could be heard. It made no difference. He had come this far, he wasn't turning back now.

A growl of triumph rose in his throat as he found an unlocked window. Luck was still smiling on him. He used cautious force to push the window upward. The protesting squeak sounded alarmingly loud. Newman paused, breathing hard. That noise sounded louder to him than it probably was.

He grasped the frame with both hands and used all his strength. The window frame must have swollen, for it rose with a loud squeak.

Newman leaned through the opening and waited. He heard no movement from inside the house. Luck was still with him. He clambered through the window, leaving it open. It might be his escape route.

Harl came back on a hard run. He was panting as he reached the house. That damned woman in the restaurant had been distressingly slow as she fixed him a couple of sandwiches.

He carried the sandwiches in a paper bag. He had no idea how long he had been gone, but it seemed forever.

The house seemed the same, but an icy feeling was stealing through him. Something was wrong. He couldn't eat the sandwiches until he had thoroughly checked out the house.

He moved slowly around it. The light in Temple's room was still on, and Harl couldn't see anything that was out of place.

He moved slowly on, not sure of what he was looking for. He stopped suddenly as he saw the open window. His heart dropped into his stomach. Something was wrong. The opened window shouted it louder than any words.

He dropped the sandwiches, forgetting all about his hunger. He climbed silently through the window. He thought he knew who the intruder was, and that lighted room would be the first place to look. He moved toward the line of light beneath the door, placing his steps carefully.

Newman stopped to ease his labored breathing. His eyes adjusted to the darkness, and he saw he was in a long hall. Doors opened off the hall, but a line of light beneath the door at the end of the hall told him that room was occupied.

He moved down the hall, his lips drawn back in anticipation. He winced every time a board creaked beneath his step.

Newman stopped with his hand on the doorknob. The beating of his heart had slowed. He had made it. He turned the knob, holding the door tightly against the jamb until the knob was completely turned. A gentle pressure opened the door noiselessly.

Newman stepped silently through it, his eyes gleaming. Temple was pacing agitatedly about the room. At the moment, his head was turned away from Newman. He must have just gotten up, for the rocking chair still moved gently. A pistol lay on the table beside the chair.

Ah, Newman thought. Temple must have been warned about my escape, and he's ready. The waiting must have worked on his nerves until he could no longer sit still.

Newman moved silently nearer to the table, until he was between it and Temple. Temple could never reach the gun first.

Newman slid the knife out of its sheath. God, the pleasure of this moment was unreal.

"Hello, Ira," he said softly. "You waiting for me?"

Temple's shoulders jerked and his back stiffened. He didn't turn immediately. Perhaps he was hoping that it was only imagination that he thought he heard a voice.

Temple turned, and his face filled with despair. "No," he said brokenly, as though the single word would drive away the apparition.

"Didn't you expect me to come back?" Newman asked

passionately. He caught himself, remembering to lower his voice.

Temple cast a measuring eye toward the gun and saw that Newman was closer. "Wait a minute, Mungo," he begged. "You've got it all wrong. I intended to come down and talk to you, but things came up. I've got the money ready. I'm going to give it to Ruby, tomorrow at the latest."

"You miserable, lying bastard," Newman raged. "You never had any intention of giving her that money. And I believed in you."

Temple glanced frantically at the gun, so close but still too far away. He retreated before Newman's remorseless advance.

"This won't do you any good, Mungo," he said hoarsely. "It'll only make things worse for you."

Temple was up against a wall, and he couldn't retreat any farther. The knife tip darted out at him, and he sucked in his belly, trying to shrink into the smallest possible space.

"This frighten you?" Newman asked tauntingly. "It should. Maybe you know a little of the fear I went through. You lied to me from the start, didn't you? You knew I wouldn't get off easy."

Temple's eyes bulged with terror. "The sentence shocked me as much as it did you, Mungo. I talked to the judge. I did everything possible to ease your sentence. Do you think I wanted this to happen to you?"

"You're damned right I do," Newman hissed. "You probably knew what was going to happen. I'm sick of listening to your lies."

Newman lunged forward, balanced on the balls of his feet, ready to go any way Temple chose.

Temple was frozen with fear. He saw the darting approach of the knife and tried to swing an arm to block it. He was too late. The blade sliced through one side of his arm. His mouth opened wide at the fierce wash of pain. The point of the knife drove ahead for its target and buried deeply into Temple's stomach.

Newman jerked the knife free and stood over Temple, his eyes crazed. He labored to breathe through his opened mouth.

Temple looked up at him, his eyes dulling. "You did it," he said in a wondering voice. "You went ahead and did it. They'll hang you for this."

"Goddamn you," Newman said hoarsely. "Shut up. This was all your doing. I'm going to cut you in such small pieces that there won't be anything to bury."

He started to lunge at Temple again when an imperative voice came from the doorway. "Hold it. Right where you are. I mean it, Newman. I'll blow your head off."

Temple was on the floor, the fingers of both hands pressed tightly against his stomach. Despite the pressure, blood spurted between his fingers.

Harl's yell got through to Newman, for he turned his head. Bewilderment washed over his face before rage swept it away. "I'm not going to prison," he growled.

"This time, you won't have to," Harl said grimly. "You'll be hanged."

All sanity left Newman. Saliva dripped from his lower lip as he said, "You're not going to take me. I'll cut you worse than I did Temple."

He advanced slowly toward Harl, the point of the knife aimed at Harl's chest. He must have forgotten all about the pistol, for he never tried to touch it.

Harl recognized the madness in Newman's eyes. He knew words wouldn't stop him, but he gave Newman a last chance. "Your last warning, Newman," he said.

Newman was across the room from Harl. It would take several strides to reach Harl, and there wasn't the slightest chance he could do it. But Newman was beyond all reason.

All he could think of was to reach Harl and drive the knife home.

Harl saw determination mold Newman's face. Newman lowered his head and lunged across the room. He hadn't taken the second step when Harl pulled the trigger. Momentum carried Newman another stride, but he was beginning to come apart. His face was set in surprised shock, and the flame in his eyes began to die.

He still struggled to cover the remaining distance between him and Harl. He fought to reach for another step, and he still held the knife.

Harl shot him a second time. At this short distance, there was no need for careful aiming.

The bullet hit Newman in the chest, and its impact flung him erect and threw him backward. There was no use shooting again. Almost instantaneously, the slackness of death was beginning to set in. He slumped to the floor, half rolled over, then was still.

Melody pounded on the door, and Harl heard her frantic cries. "What's happening in there?" she begged.

Harl sighed as he moved to open the door. He didn't want her seeing all this, but he didn't see how he could avoid it. He thought he heard cries from outside of the house and hoped the noise of gun reports had reached other people, too. He wanted Quincy Rader to get here as fast as he could make it.

Chapter Twenty-eight

Temple was dying. There was no mistaking it. His voice was so faint that Harl could scarcely hear it. Melody was seated beside her brother, his head in her lap.

Melody was made of stern stuff. She gasped at the sight of Temple, lying in a pool of blood, and color rushed out of her face. Harl was sure she would faint. But she had shaken off the weakness and gone to her brother.

"Will that doctor ever come?" Melody cried in growing despair.

"He's on his way, Melody," Harl answered. "Just hold on." He grimaced. Temple was the one who should be encouraged to hold on.

The gun shots had attracted outsiders, and Harl sent one of them to Ruby's house to get Quincy. After that, he had firmly closed the door in all those inquisitive faces.

Rader talked in a low voice with Harl. "I was wrong, Harl. I thought he'd try to get to Ruby first."

Harl shook his head. "He was too eaten up by hate, Quincy. He might have made it, but he opened a window and crawled into the house. In his anxiety to get at Temple, he forgot to close the window."

Rader scowled at Newman's body. "Did he say anything that made sense?"

"No, Quincy. He was completely out of his mind. He was wearing a gun, but he forgot all about it. His only thought was to use the knife on me."

"Where is that doctor?" Melody cried again.

Temple coughed, and his voice had faded to a mere whisper. "It wouldn't make any difference, Melody. If the doctor had been here from the first, it wouldn't do any good."

"You mustn't talk," she said softly. "You cannot afford the strength."

His attempt at a smile twisted into a horrible contortion of pain. "Don't worry, Melody. All of this is my fault." At her widening eyes he nodded feebly. "It is. I know it's made a breach between you and Harl. I can't let that continue."

He went into a coughing spell again. Each paroxysm further weakened him, and he spoke faster as though he were racing time. "I wanted to be a bigger man than I've ever been, Melody. I thought acquiring land was the surest way to accomplish that." He coughed again, and she held his head to ease the pain. "I wanted a lot of land, Melody. I knew the winter had put Hiram Stark in trouble, and he wouldn't be able to make his annual payment. Hiram was noted for an explosive temper. If he lost that temper and threatened me, a hired guard would have every right to shoot him." His head sagged, and his eyes closed. Melody tried to fight off the terrible fear he was gone.

His eyes reopened, and he resumed his story in a faltering, reedy voice. "Newman was in arrears of his payment, and he jumped at the offer of a job. I built him up with stories about Hiram. He was sure if he shot Hiram he wouldn't be charged with anything more serious than self-defense. The judge didn't see the trial that way. You heard the sentence he gave Newman."

"You've talked too much," Melody said, anguish threatening to break through her defense.

"Not quite enough," Temple said. His voice was so low, she had to bend her head close to hear him. "I foreclosed on Harl. Harl's ranch doesn't belong to the bank. I want you to tell him—" his voice suddenly snapped off, and his eyes remained open, fixed and staring.

Perhaps it was the dreadful looseness of his body that told Melody he was gone. "Ira," she called. She repeated his name until she was convinced there would be no response. Her sobbing came then, great shaking waves of grief.

Harl turned at the sound of her uncontrollable weeping. "He's gone," he said flatly. "I'm surprised he lasted this long. We've got to get her away from him."

Rader nodded agreement. "Wonder what he was talking about," he mused.

"Only Melody knows," Harl replied. "Unless she wants to tell us, we'll never know."

Together, they gently pried Melody's hold from her brother's body. She resisted being led away.

"We'll take care of him, Melody," Harl kept saying. "It's best this way."

They finally got her out of the room. Harl found a woman neighbor in the group of people outside and turned Melody over to her.

"She's had an awful shock, Mrs. Brown. Maybe some hot coffee will help her."

Mrs. Brown's ample arm was about Melody's shoulders. "I'll take care of her."

Harl nodded soberly. Mrs. Brown was one of those dependable kind of people.

He watched them walk away and said bleakly, "It's been a bad night, Quincy." The echoes of Temple's ambition had gone full cycle, culminating in his own death.

"It's not quite over, Harl," Rader said quietly. At Harl's questioning frown, he said, "Somebody has to tell Ruby."

"Oh, God," Harl moaned. Ruby's grief would probably be deeper, more intense, for the love between a man and a wife was different than that between a brother and sister. Harl was fearful that Rader would send him on this dreadful errand.

"I'll do it," Rader said.

A sigh escaped Harl. "I'd sure appreciate that, Quincy."

They went out of the house together, pushing their way through the last of the inquisitive neighbors. Rader said as an afterthought, "You better tell Wilkie to pick up Ira and Newman."

Harl nodded grimly. A night like this seemed never to end. "I'll tell him, Quincy."

Chapter Twenty-nine

Rader didn't come in until late in the morning. Harl supposed he was trying to make up some of his lost sleep. Last night had been a hectic one.

"Rough?" Harl asked sympathetically.

Rader sighed. "I don't want to go through that every night. I thought Ruby was going to scream until she lost her senses." He was reflectively silent a moment. "That woman really cared for Mungo Newman."

Two women had known grief last night, and neither had earned it.

"What did you do with her, Quincy?"

"I sent for a doctor. He gave her something that knocked her out. That'll hold her until late in the day. But what does she do then, Harl?"

Harl spread his hands. He didn't have enough wisdom to answer that question.

"Did Wilkie pick up Ira?" Rader asked.

Harl nodded. "I waited until he came. He took Newman, too." He guessed at the question in Rader's eyes. "I didn't see Melody again. If she was asleep, I didn't want to awaken her. Sleep would do her more good than anything I could say."

"Yes," Rader agreed absently. "Two different women," he remarked.

Harl knew what he meant. Melody was tough. Much like Addie, he thought, where poor Ruby was defenseless. Melody could absorb this blow and go on living. He wondered what would become of Ruby.

He stared across the room, and Rader asked, "What's got you in such a deep study?"

"I was thinking of what Hiram said. About an echo coming from everything that happens. He sure was right, wasn't he?"

Rader didn't answer, and Harl looked at him. Rader stared at the front door, and Harl turned his head. Melody was just entering.

Harl jumped to his feet. Her swollen eyes showed how much crying she had done, but all in all, Harl would say she was bearing up remarkably well.

"Melody, you shouldn't be up and around this early," he protested.

A wave of her hand swept his words aside. "Too many things to do, Harl."

"But couldn't somebody do them for you? I'd be glad to do whatever I can."

Her smile had only a semblance of its former radiance. "I know you would, Harl. But some things I have to do myself. The big one is the reason I'm here."

Harl watched her take a chair, his face puzzled. He had no idea what the big thing was or why she was here.

"Ira talked to me before he died," she said painfully. She looked directly at him. "Harl, Ira was responsible for all this trouble. He wanted to own the Bow Gun. He knew if Hiram missed a payment, he could take over."

Harl sat stiffly upright. This was distressing Melody. Maybe she felt family shame.

"Take your time," he said softly.

Melody shook her head. She had started, and no matter how difficult it was, she intended to finish.

"Ira was afraid of Hiram's temper. If he took the Bow Gun, Hiram could jump him. He figured a guard would protect him. He hired Newman. Newman was slow thinking. If he could be convinced Hiram's temper was a threat, he might be tricked into shooting Hiram. Newman was under obligation to Ira, and he was grateful for his job."

Harl's eyes burned, but he managed to keep his "ah" under control.

"Ira figured Newman would be acquitted on self-defense." Melody lifted her hands and let them fall helplessly. "I'm sorry, Harl." She was very close to tears again. "If you'll come to the bank, I'll return your mortgage. The bank doesn't want property acquired that way."

Of course, she didn't, Harl thought. But Ira certainly had. Naturally, Melody would inherit the bank. What a vast difference a change in ownership would make in that bank.

Her face clouded as she misread his sternness. "You don't think I'd want that ranch, do you?" Tears glistened in her eyes. "I don't even know what to do with the bank. I don't know how to run it."

Harl grinned. That was enough to give an untrained woman something to worry about. "You don't have to run it, Melody. Charley Duncan can do that for you."

Her eyes widened as though this was an entirely new thought. "Do you think he'd consider it?" she asked doubtfully.

"He'd jump at the opportunity," Harl assured her. "He's waited a lot of years for just such a chance."

Relief flooded her face. "Do you really think he would take the job?"

"Believe it," Harl said solemnly.

Her expression was akin to happiness. "I'm going to find him and ask. Oh, Harl, you don't know what you've done for me."

He walked with her to the door. "You don't know what you've done for me," he said.

She paused at the door. "Harl, I'd like to offer Ruby twenty-five hundred dollars. She had no part in this. Do you think I would offend her?"

"No," Harl answered stoutly. "You're doing a fine thing, Melody. It's not your responsibility."

She looked squarely at him. "You will come down to the bank?"

"Count on it." Harl intended to see her far more often than just a brief visit at the bank.

"Jesus," Rader said softly when Harl returned from the door. "I never thought it would wind up like this."

"Me, neither," Harl said happily. "There's all kinds of echoes, Quincy. I guess Hiram didn't figure on there being good ones, too."

Rader nodded. "Kinda restores a man's faith." He watched Harl unpin his badge. "What's this?" he exclaimed.

"I'm quitting, Quincy. I've got a ranch to run."

Rader looked dolefully at the badge Harl laid on his desk. "Figures," he said, "but I'm not happy about it."

Harl reached for Rader's hand and wrung it hard. "I'm grateful to you in more ways than one. I don't know what I'd have done without this job."

"Nothing to thank me for," Rader grumbled. "You earned your way. Without you, I might still be picking at the problem." His voice was husky, and he didn't fully meet Harl's eyes. "What are your plans, Harl?"

"I've got to stop by the bank and pick up some papers, then I'm going home."

"You'll be back to see Melody more often?" Rader asked with a shine in his eyes.

"I don't think so, Quincy." Harl broke into a chuckle at the surprise crossing Rader's face. "I'm going to talk her into going home with me. Ma will be tickled. And I don't want Melody living alone in that big house."

Rader grinned wryly. "You know something, Harl? I think you'll do just that. You're a pretty hardheaded man when it comes to getting your way."

"I hope you're right, Quincy." Harl walked to the door, turned there, and flashed the brightest grin Rader had ever seen.